A Death in the Country

A DEATH IN THE COUNTRY

AND OTHER TALES OF OUR TIME

STEPHEN VINCENT BENÉT

2015

A Death in the Country was first published in 1932, *Too Early Spring* in 1933, *The Story About the Anteater* in 1928, *Schooner Fairchild's Class* in 1938, *Everybody was Very Nice* in 1936, *All Around the Town* in 1940, *Glamour* in 1932, *No Visitors* in 1940. The first collection of these stories under the title *Tales of Our Time* first appeared in *Selected Works of Steven Vincent Benét,* vol. 2, published by Farrar & Rinehart, 1942.

CONTENTS

A Death in the Country

A Death in the Country

(1932)

AFTER THE YEARS, Tom Carroll was going back to Waynesville—to stand by a kinswoman's grave, in the country of his
youth. The names of the small, familiar stations were knots on a
thread that led back into the darkness of childhood. He was glad
Claire had not come. She hated death and memories. She hated
cramped, local trains that smelled of green plush and cinders.
Most of all she would hate Waynesville, even in mid-September
and the grave light of afternoon.

Well, he wasn't looking forward to a pleasant time. He felt
fagged and on edge already. There was work for the active partner of Norman, Buckstone, and Carroll in his brief-case, but he
could not get down to the work. Instead he remembered, from
childhood, the smell of dyed cloth and poignant, oppressive
flowers, the black wisp tied on the knocker, the people coming
to the door. The house was full of a menace—full of a secret—
there were incomprehensible phrases, said in a murmur, and a
man in black gloves who came, and a strangeness behind a shut
door. Run out and play, run out and play; but there was no right
way to play any more—even out in the yard you could smell the
sweet, overpowering flowers—even out in the street you could
see the people coming and coming, making that little pause as
they saw the black wisp. Beautiful, they said, she looks beautiful; but the glimpse of the face was not mother, only somebody

coldly asleep. Our sister has gone to dear Jesus... we shall meet on that beautiful shore... but the man spoke words, and the harsh box sank into the hole, and from it nothing arose, not even a white thing, not even silver vapor; the clay at the sides of the hole was too yellow and thick and cold. He's too young to realize, said a great many voices—but for months nothing was right. The world had stopped being solid, and people's smiles were different, and mother was Jesus's sister, and they gave her clothes away. Then, after a long time, the place was green again and looked just like the other graves, and the knife in your pocket was a comfort, going out there Sundays in the street car.

Barbarous. And to-morrow would be barbarous, as well. The family met only at funerals and weddings, now; and there had been more funerals than weddings for the past ten years. The big Christmas tree was gone from the house on Hessian Street—the majestic tree whose five-pointed, sparkling star had scratched against the ceiling of heaven in the back parlor, spreading wide its green boughs to shelter all generations and tribes of the Pyes and Merritts and Chipmans, their wives and their children, their menservants and their maidservants, their Noah's arks and cigar-cases and bottles of *eau-de-cologne*. The huge tablecloth of Thanksgiving lay folded away at the bottom of a chest—the tables now were too small. There would never be another turkey, with a breast like a mountainside, to fall into endless slices under the shining magic of Uncle Melrose's knife. Aunt Louise and Aunt Emmy had been the last of Hessian Street and, after to-morrow, there would only be Aunt Emmy and the ghosts.

The faces around the table had been masterful and full of life. They had been grown-up and permanent—one could not imagine them young or growing old. Together, they made a nation; they were the earth. If one took the trains of the morning, even as far as Bradensburg, lo, Uncle Melrose was there, at his desk with the little brass postage-scale on top of it, as it had been from the first. If one walked out to Mount Pleasant through the buckeye fall, at the end there was the white gate of Cousin Edna and the iron nigger boy with the rain-streaked face, holding out his black hand stiffly for the buckboards that drove no more. There were princes and dominations and thrones and powers; but what were these beside Aunt Emmy and Cousin Millie, beside the everlasting forms of Mrs. Bache and Mr. Beaver, of the ladies at the Women's Exchange and the man who lighted the gas street-lamps with a long brass spike? Then, suddenly, the earth had begun to crumble. A wind blew, a bell sounded, and they were dispersed. There were shrunken old people, timorous and pettish, and a small, heart-stifling town. These and the grown-up children, more strange than strangers. But Hessian Street was over—the great tree was down.

"And Uncle Melrose was a pompous old windbag," thought Tom Carroll. "And yet, if he were alive, I'd be calling him 'Sir.' Oh, Claire's right—the jungle's the jungle—she's saner than I am, always."

It was one of the many maxims Claire found in books. The family was the jungle that you grew up in and, if you did not, somehow, break through to light and air of your own when you were young, you died, quickly or slowly but surely, stifled out, choked down by the overpowering closeness of your own kin. Tom Carroll knew this much—that New York, after Waynesville, had been like passing from the large, squabbling, over-heated room of Christmas afternoon into the anonymous peace of a bare and windy street. He had been lonely, often—he had missed Hessian Street and them all. But, oh the endless, intricate, unimportant diplomacy—the feuds and the makings-up—the inflexible machine of the Family, crushing all independence. Not again, not ever again! And yet, here he was, on the train.

Well, nobody could say that he shirked it. He would have to take charge when he got there, like it or not. It wouldn't be easy, straightening everything out—he'd rather handle the Corliss case any day—but he'd done it in other emergencies and he supposed he could do it again. After all, who else was there? Jerry Pye? His mouth narrowed, thinking of Jerry.

The conductor bawled the names of familiar stations, the long, autumnal twilight began beyond the window. If only things could go smoothly just this once! But something always cropped up—something always had to be smoothed over and explained. *Morton Center, Morton Center!* If Aunt Louise had left no will—and she very probably hadn't—there'd be the dickens of a time, securing the estate to Aunt Emmy. But it must be done—he'd ride roughshod over Jerry Pye if necessary. *Brandy Hill! Brandy Hill!* ... If only nobody would tell him to be sure and notice Mrs. Bache! He could easily fix a pension for Aunt Emmy, but how to do it best? She'd have to leave Hessian Street, of course. Even cutting the old house into apartments hadn't really solved the problem. She could get a small, comfortable, modern flat over in the new section. The silver candlesticks were the only things Claire would have liked, but they would go to Jerry because Jerry had always failed.

Waynesville, next stop! The flowers had been wired from New York. *Waynesville!* We're coming in. There's an A.&P. on Main Street, and Ellerman's Bazaar is gone. *Waynesville!*... And God bless Uncle Melrose and Aunt Louise and Aunt Emmy and all my dear relations and friends and Spot and make me a good boy and not afraid of the dark. *Waynesville!*

Right down the middle of Main Street the train clanged till it stopped in front of the bald, new station. Tom Carroll sighed. It was as he had prophesied. Jerry Pye was there to meet him.

He got off the train, and the cousins shook hands.

"Have a good trip, Tom?"

"Not bad. Real fall weather, isn't it?"

"Yes, it's a real fall. You took the limited as far as Bradensburg, I suppose?"

"Yes, that seemed the quickest thing for me to do."

"They say she's quite a train," said Jerry Pye. "I was on her once—three years ago, you know. Well, I thought, here's where the old man blows himself for once. Minnie would hardly believe me when I told her. 'Jerry Pye!' she said, 'I don't know what's come over you. You never take me on any limiteds!' 'Well,' I said, 'maybe it is extra-fare, but I just decided the old man could blow himself for once!' Well, you should have seen her expression! Though I guess it wouldn't mean much to you, at that. I guess extra-fare trains don't mean much in people's lives when they come from New York."

"I could have taken a slower train," said Tom Carroll, carefully, "but it wouldn't have saved any time."

This remark seemed to amuse Jerry Pye intensely. His thin, sallow face—the face of a dyspeptic fox—gloated with mirth for an instant. Then he sobered himself, abruptly and pointedly.

"You always were a case, Tom," he said, "always. But this is a sad occasion."

"I didn't mean to be funny," said Tom Carroll. "Had I better get a taxi or is that your car?"

"Oh, we've got the family mistake—a dollar down and a dollar whenever they catch you!" Jerry Pye grinned and sobered himself again with the automatism of a mechanical figure. "I drove up in her night before last," he said, pointedly, as they got in. "Evans is a good man and all that, but he's apt to figure a little close on the cars; and as long as ours is dark blue, it'll look perfectly dignified."

"I telegraphed Aunt Emmy," said Tom Carroll and stopped.

There was no possible use in trying to explain oneself to Jerry Pye.

"Yes, indeed," said Jerry, instantly. "Aunt Emmy appreciated it very much. Very much indeed. 'Tom's always very busy,' I told her. 'But don't you worry, Aunt Emmy. Tom may be a big man now, but his heart's in the right place. He'll be here.'"

"I told her," said Tom Carroll, distinctly and in spite of himself, "that in case anything of the sort came up, she had only to—"

"Oh," said Jerry, brightly, "we all knew that. We all knew you couldn't be expected to send one of your big cars all the way from New York to Waynesville. How's Claire?"

"Claire was very sorry indeed not to be able to come," said Tom, his hands gripping his knees. "We have one car," he said.

"That's just what I said," said Jerry Pye triumphantly. "I told Aunt Emmy—'you couldn't expect Tom to take the car away from Claire—she'll need it when he's away, shopping and seeing her friends—and naturally she hardly knew Aunt Louise. You wait and see. She'll send handsome flowers,' I said."

"Oh, God, make me a good boy!" prayed Tom Carroll, internally. "It can't last more than ten minutes. Ten minutes isn't really long." He braced himself. "How is Aunt Emmy?" he said.

Their speed instantly dropped to a respectful twenty miles an hour.

"She's wonderful," said Jerry Pye. "Simply wonderful. Of course, Minnie's been a great help to her and then, the end was very peaceful. Just seemed to breathe away." His voice had an obvious relish. "One minute she was there—as bright as a button, considering everything—and the next minute—" He shook his head.

"I'm glad," said Tom Carroll. "I mean—"

"Oh, we wouldn't have wanted her to suffer," said Jerry Pye in a shocked voice, as if he were denying some uncouth suggestion of Tom's. "No, sir, we wouldn't have wanted that. Now when Minnie's mother passed over—I don't know whether I ever told you the whole story, Tom—but from the Friday before—"

He continued, but had only come to the personal idiosyncrasies of the first night nurse when they turned into Hessian Street.

They got out of the car. Jerry Pye was mopping his forehead, though the day was chill. Yes, there was the black wisp on the knocker. But there was a row of bell-pushes where the old name-plate had been. The bricks in the sidewalk were rose-red and old and worn—the long block of quiet houses kept its faded dignity, in spite of a sign, "Pappas' Smoke Shop," a sign, "The Hessian Sergeant—Tea and Antiques." The linden trees had not perished, though their shade was thin.

"If this were a city," thought Tom Carroll, "people would have found out by now that it was quaint and painted the doors green and had studio-parties. Well, anyhow, that hasn't happened."

"Everyone's been very respectful," said Jerry Pye, nodding at the black wisp. "I mean, some people might be touchy when everybody has to use the same front-door. But Mr. Rodman came to me himself—they're the second-floor back. Just leave your bag in the car, Tom. It won't be in the way. I think Minnie's seen us— we figured out if you came to-day this ought to be the train."

Tom Carroll did not repeat that he had telegraphed or that there was only one afternoon train to Waynesville. He kissed his cousin-in-law's flustered cheek and was kissed by her in return. Minnie was always flustered; she had been a plump, flustered robin of a girl at her wedding; she was unaltered now save for the dust of gray in her abundant, unbecoming hair; they had never exchanged three words, except on family matters; and yet, they always kissed. He wondered if Minnie, too, ever found this circumstance strange. He should not wonder, of course, especially now.

"How's Aunt Emmy?" said Jerry Pye, in the anxious tones of one just returned from a long absence. "There isn't any change?"

"No, dear," said Minnie, solemnly, "she's just the same. She's wonderful. Mrs. Robinson and Mrs. Bache are with her, now. Remember—we must all be very nice to Mrs. Bache, Cousin Tom."

"I did put a tick-tack on her window, once," said Tom Carroll, reflectively. "But I haven't done that for a long time. Not for thirty years."

Minnie, the robin, was shocked for a moment, but brightened.

"That's right," she said. "We must all keep up for Aunt Emmy. Now, if you'll just go in—" She stood aside.

The spare, small, hawk-nosed figure rose from the stiff-backed chair as Tom Carroll entered. "Good evening, Thomas. I am glad you are here," said the unfaltering voice. "I think you know my good neighbors, Mrs. Bache and Mrs. Robinson."

Tom Carroll took the thin, dry, forceful hands. By God, she is wonderful, he thought, in spite of their saying it—it's taken me years to unlearn what she taught me, but she's remarkable. Why don't they let her alone? *Aunt Emmy, Aunt Emmy, you have grown so small! You rapped on my chapped knuckles with a steel thimble when I was cold; you ran me through and through like the emery-bag in your workbox with your sharp and piercing eyes; you let me see that you thought my father a rascal; you made me lie and cheat because of the terror of your name—and now you have grown small and fragile and an old woman, and there is not even injustice left in Hessian Street.*

The moment passed. Tom Carroll found himself mechanically answering Mrs. Bache's questions while his eyes roved about the room. The conch-shell was still on the mantelpiece, but one of the blue vases was gone. This was the front-parlor—the room of reward and punishment, of visitors and chill, the grandest room in the world—this room with the shabby carpet and the huge forbidding pieces of black walnut that never could have come in through a mortal door. What could you do with it all, what could you do? What could be done with a conch-shell and an iron oak-leaf and a set of yellowed pictures for a broken stereopticon? It was incredible that civilized people should ever have cherished such things. It was incredible that he had ever put the conch-shell to his ear and held his breath with wonder, hearing the sea.

"It was just like another home to the Major and myself. Always," said Mrs. Bache. "I can hear your dear grandmother now, before the Major was taken, when he had his trouble. 'Alice, my child, you're young,' she said. 'But, young or old, we all have to bear our cross. The Major is a good man—he'll always be welcome in Hessian Street.' The Major never forgot it. He was very badly treated but he never forgot a kindness. And now, Emmy and I are the last—Emmy and I are the last."

She fumbled for her handkerchief in her vast lap.

"There, there, Mrs. Bache," said Tom Carroll, inadequately, "Grandmother must have been a wonderful woman."

"You never even saw her," said Mrs. Bache, viciously, "Tom Carroll saw to that. Oh, why couldn't it have been me, instead of Louise?" she said. "I've been ready to go so long!"

Tom Carroll's face felt stiff, but he found the handkerchief. After a moment Mrs. Bache arose, enormously yet with a curious dignity.

"Come, Sarah," she said to the dim figure in black that was Mrs. Robinson, "It's time for us to go. I've been making a fool of myself. Good-by, Emma. Frank will take us to the church to-morrow. Try to get some rest."

Minnie was whispering to him that Mrs. Bache was very

much broken and that Cousin Tom must not mind. Tom Carroll whispered back at appropriate intervals. He did not mind Mrs. Bache. But there was always so much whispering, and it hurt one's head.

Now they were all standing in the narrow hall, and the others were looking at him.

"We can just slip in for a minute before anyone else comes," whispered Minnie, "I know Cousin Tom would rather—"

"Of course," said Tom Carroll. "Thank you, Cousin Minnie." He must have been working too hard, he thought—perhaps he and Claire could go off for a trip together when he got back. Because, after all, it was Aunt Louise who was dead. He knew that perfectly well. And yet, until Minnie had spoken, he hadn't been thinking about her at all.

The statue lay on the walnut bed in the partitioned room that had once been part of the back parlor. Over the head of the bed was a cross of dry, brittle palm-leaves tied with a purple ribbon, and a church-calendar. Against the opposite wall was the highboy that he remembered, with the small china slipper upon it, and above it the ageless engraving of the great Newfoundland dog, head lifted, lying upon the stone blocks of an English quay. "A Member of the Royal Humane Society." There were brown spots on the margin of the engraving now, Tom Carroll noticed. The window was a little open, but everywhere were the massed, triumphant flowers.

A white, transparent veil lay on the face of the statue. The features showed dimly through it, as if Aunt Louise lay in a block of ice. Tom Carroll felt cold. Now Aunt Emmy, putting Minnie aside, went slowly to lift the veil.

Tom Carroll, waking at three o'clock in the morning in his room at the Penniquit House, knew instantly what was in store for him. He might lie on the hillocks of his bed as long as he liked but he would not be allowed to sleep any more.

"You're acting like somebody on the edge of a first-class nervous breakdown," he told himself sternly. "And yet, you haven't been working so hard."

The last year hadn't been easy, but no year was. When times were good, you worked hard to take advantage of them. And when they were bad, you naturally had to work. That was how you got to be some body, in a city. It was something Waynesville could never understand.

He thought of their life in the city—his and Claire's—for solace. It was cool and glittering and civilized as a cube of bright steel and glass. He thought of the light, pleasant furniture in the apartment, the clean, bright colors, the crisp sunlight on stone and metal, the bright, clean, modern, expensive school where a doctor looked down the boys' throats every morning and they had special blocks of wood to hammer nails in, since apartments were hardly the places to hammer nails. He thought of his office and the things on his desk and the crowded elevators of morning and night. He thought of the crammed red moving vans of October and the spring that bloomed before April in the flower-shops and the clever men, putting in the new telephones. He thought of night beside Claire, hearing the dim roar of the city till at last the uneasy lights of the sky were quieted in the breathing-space before dawn.

It was she who had really held their life to its pattern. She had not let them be trapped; she had kept them free as air from the first day. There had been times when he had weakened—he admitted it—but she had kept her level head and never given in.

It had been that way about the old farmhouse in Connecticut and the cooperative apartment in town. He had wanted to buy them both, at different times. It was the Waynesville coming out in him, he supposed. But she had demurred.

"Oh, Tom, let's not tie ourselves up yet!" she had said. "Yes, I know it does seem silly just going on paying rent and having nothing to show for it but a leak in the washstand. But the minute you buy places to live in, they start to own you. You aren't free. You aren't young. You're always worrying. Don't talk to me about just playing with a few acres, not really farming. That was the way Grandfather started. Oh, Tom, don't you see—we're so *right* the way we are! Now, let's go over it sensibly, figures and all."

And she had been right. The old farmhouse, with its lilac hedge, now stood twenty feet away from a four-lane road; the cooperative apartment had failed and crippled its owner-tenants. She had been precisely right. She almost always was.

She had been entirely and unsentimentally right about her mother's coming to live with them for six months out of the year, when that had seemed unescapable.

"It's darling of you, Tom, but, dear old man, it never would work in the world. We've got to be modern and intelligent about the important things. Mother had me, and I'm devoted to her; but, when we're together for more than a week we get on each other's nerves like the very devil. It'll actually be a help to Hattie to have her for the winters—Hattie's always having a fearful time with the children. And we can have her for a long visit in the summer, and in between she can take the trips she's always wanted to take with that terrible Mrs. Tweed. Of course, I don't mean we ought to leave the whole financial end to Hattie and Joe. I'll insist on our doing our share. But I do think people ought to have *some* independence even when they are old and not just be shipped around from one relative to another like parcels, the way they did with Aunt Vi! It's more than sweet of you, Tom, darling. But you see how it is."

Tom Carroll had seen, with some relief, that they were not likely to have Mrs. Fanshawe as a permanent addition to their household, and he had acquiesced. Not that he disliked Mrs. Fanshawe. He got on very well with the rather nervous little lady—which was strange, considering how unlike she was to Claire. It struck him at times that Mrs. Fanshawe, from what he knew of her, had never been a remarkably independent person, and that to begin one's complete independence at the age of sixty-seven might be something of a task. But Claire must know her mother better than he did.

She did get on Claire's nerves and she did spoil the children—he could see that plainly enough. But, then, her visits were seldom very long. Claire would hardly have time to decline three or four invitations because mother was with them for a quiet little time before something would happen to call Mrs. Fanshawe away. And yet she seemed to like his calling her Mother May and pretending he was jealous of Hattie and Joe for stealing away his best girl. She'd laugh her brisk, nervous laugh and say he'd better look out or sometime she'd take him at his word and stay forever. And Claire would be saying, patiently, "Now, mother, are you sure that you have your ticket? And Tom will get you some magazines to read on the train." Afterwards Claire would say, "Oh, Tom, how can you? But she adores it!" and he would mumble something and feel rather pleased. Then Claire would kiss him and go to the telephone.

Only one of the visits had been in the least unfortunate. Claire had been tired that evening, and it was a pity that the conversation had happened to run on the future of the children. "But, of course, you and Tom are planning to make a real home for them sometime?" Mrs. Fanshawe had said. Well, naturally, she could hardly be expected to understand the way he and Claire happened to feel about "homes" in the Waynesville sense.

And it had all come right the following morning—had not Mrs. Fanshawe nervously stayed an extra two days in proof? But the evening had carried him back to the hurt feelings of Hessian Street. Tom Carroll was glad there had been another visit before Mrs. Fanshawe died.

She had died in the waiting room of the Auburndale Station, on her way back to Hattie's, after a pleasant month with her old friend, Mrs. Tweed. Even so, she had been considerate; for the station agent knew her and got hold of the Morrises at once—there had been some mix-up about her telegram. Later, they had found out that she had known about her heart trouble for some time.

He had expected to take Claire on to the funeral, but Claire had been adamant. "I will not have you do it, Tom. It'll be bad enough by myself. But I will not have you mixed up in it—it isn't fair. We can have bad memories separately, but I won't have us have them together." She had grown almost hysterical about it—Claire! And so she had gone alone.

He had been very much worried till she returned, with a white changed face that refused to give any details of those three days. "Don't ask me, Tom. I've told you everything I can—oh, yes, everybody was kind and they had her hymns… but, oh Tom, it's so terrible. Terrible. The most barbarous, the most humiliating custom I know! I'll tell you this right now, I'm not going to wear mourning. I don't believe in it and I won't submit to it. All the black dresses—mother didn't really like black. Oh, Tom, Tom, when I die don't dare wear mourning for me!"

He had got her to bed and quieted at last. But she had not been herself—the true Claire—for months afterward, though, as soon as she could, she had taken up the strands of their life again and woven the pattern even more deftly and swiftly, as if each new thread were precious and each second not to be recalled.

Naturally, then, it was only right for him to come to this death in his own country alone. Any other course would have been a monstrous selfishness. And yet he wished that he could go to sleep.

Perhaps, if he thought once more of that shining cube of steel and glass that was their planned security, sleep would come. Even death in New York was different and impersonal. Except for the very mighty, it was an anonymous affair. The man in 10B died and, the next fall, they redecorated the apartment for other tenants. In a month or so even the doorman had forgotten; the newsdealer wrote another name on the morning papers. A name dropped out of the 'phone book... you had moved again, with October... moved to another city—the city at the sprawling edge of town where lie the streets and avenues of the number-less, quickly buried dead. There, too, you would be part of the crowd, and your neighbors would be strangers, as it had been in life. Your dwelling would be well kept-up, for that was written in the contract. No ghosts could ever arise from that suburban earth. For this, John Merritt and Samuel Pye had built a house in the wilderness to be a shelter and a refuge for them and their seed to the generations of generations. It was just.

Something cracked in the shining cube of glass and steel. The girders crunched on one another, wrenching apart; the glass tumbled into nothingness, falling a long way. There was nothing left but the perplexed, forgotten spirit, roused out of long sleep at last to strive, unprepared, against its immortal adversary.

Claire was all right, but she was afraid of death. He was all right, but he was afraid of death. The clever people they knew were entirely right, but most of them were deadly afraid of death.

If the life they led was rich—if it was the good life—why were they so afraid? It was not because they so joyed in all things under the sun that it was bitter to leave them. That was mortal and understandable, that had always been. But this was a blinder fear.

It had not been in sorrow or remorse that Claire had grieved for her mother. She had grieved the most because she had been afraid. And that made Claire a monster, which she was not. But there was something in it, all the same. He could admit it in her because he could admit it in himself. He lay sleepless, dreading the morrow. And yet he was not a coward so far as he knew.

They had won, but where was the victory? They had escaped from Waynesville and Hessian Street, from Fanshawe and Pye and Merritt, but where was the escape? If they were afraid in these years, how were they to deal with the years to come? Tom Carroll heard the clock in the courthouse strike five strokes. And then, when it seemed to him he could never sleep again, he fell asleep.

They drove at the slow pace down Hessian Street into Main, through the bright, morning sunlight. Tom Carroll felt ashamed of the dreams and waking of the night. He had never felt more solid and confident and assured than he did now, sitting beside Aunt Emmy, his tact and his shoulder ready for her the moment the inevitable breakdown came. Thank God! Jerry Pye was driving his own car. Jerry muddled things so. As for what was to come, that would merely be pathetic—the few old people painfully come together to mourn not only one of their own but a glory that had departed, the Waynesville of their youth. He hoped Aunt Emmy would not notice how few they were. But she, too, was old; and the old lived in the past. She could people the empty pews with the faces that once had been there. It was better so. The lords of Hessian and Bounty Streets had ruled the town with a high hand, even as they sank into poverty, but that was ended. You had only to look along Main to see the new names on the shop-fronts. They knew not Hessian Street, these Caprellos and Szukalskis, but they thrived and inherited the land. Even Waynesville was growing up—there was little charm left in it, but it was alive. And here was the old brick church of the memories.

He helped Aunt Emmy expertly from the car, but she would not take his arm. Well, he respected her courage. He stood tactfully to shield her from the sight of the coffin, just being lifted down from that other, windowless car. But before he knew it Jerry Pye was beside them.

"Aunt Emmy," said Jerry Pye incredibly, "did Aunt Louise really want old Zenas to be one of the coffin-bearers? Because he's there now, and it'll be too late unless somebody tells him…"

He actually made a gesture with his hand. Tom Carroll would have been glad to strangle his cousin. But miraculously Aunt Emmy did not break.

She even walked past Tom Carroll to look deliberately at the six black-suited negroes who now had their burden ready to carry into the church. Tom Carroll looked as well. They were none of them under forty, and their faces were grave and sober, but there was something ceremonial in their attitude that struck Tom Carroll strangely. They were sad but they were not constrained—they were doing something they felt to be right and they did it naturally and with ceremony. They would remember the ceremony always when the sadness had passed.

"Zenas, Joram, Joseph, William, Henry, Devout," said Aunt Emmy, in a half-whisper. "Yes, that's right. That's right. Zenas should be there. Louise would have missed Zenas. No, Tommy, we will let them pass, please."

When the coffin had passed, to the sway of the easy shoulders, they followed it in. It was the beginning of Tom Carroll's astonishment. The astonishment did not lessen when he found the church half full, and not only with the old.

He had always thought of Aunt Louise as Aunt Emmy's shadow—in his boyhood as someone always hurried but vaguely sweet whose peppermint-drops took away the taste of Aunt Emmy's wrath; in his manhood as a responsibility at the back of his mind. But the minister was a young man, and neither Pye nor Merritt, and he spoke of the Louise Pye, whose single-handed effort had turned the ramshackle old School For The Instruction Of Freed Negroes into an institution model for its time, in terms that assumed his hearers knew and appreciated the difficulties of that task.

Phrases came to Tom Carroll's ears. They were the conventional phrases of oratory, yet the speaker meant them. "Unsparing of time or labor." "The rare gift of personality." "The quiet achievement of many years." "We can say to-day, in all truth, a light has gone from among us...." But this was Aunt Louise!

And after the service, and on the way to the grave, and after the service there, the astonishment continued. He was by Aunt Emmy's side, and the people spoke to him. Nearly everyone who spoke to him knew his name. They did not find it odd or kind or a favor that he should be there—he was Julia Merritt's son, who was working in New York. You didn't hear as much about him as you did about Jerry Pye, but it was natural that he should return. Not only Mrs. Bache was under the impression that he had come principally to hear the reading of Aunt Louise's will. They did not think ill of him for it, merely prudent. He could explain nothing, even if he had wished to. There was nothing to explain.

He could not count the number of times he was told that the cross of yellow roses was beautiful—did they know by telepathy that it was from him and Claire? He had thought it garish and out of place beside the other flowers, the late asters and first chrysanthemums, the zinnias and snapdragons, the bronzes and reds and golds of the country fall. But that he could not say.

The negroes who had borne the coffin knew him. They spoke to him gravely in their rich voices when all was done. Aunt Emmy had a curious phrase for each of them. "Thank you, Devout. Thank you, Joram. Miss Louise will be pleased." It would seem macabre, telling it to Claire. It was not; it was only simple. But that she would not believe.

He remembered, as if in a dream, his plans for succor and comfort when Aunt Emmy should collapse. But it was he who felt physically exhausted when they got back to the house.

This, too, was the moment that he had dreaded the most. Last night he had been able to have dinner at the hotel, but this time there was no escaping the cold meal laid in the basement dining room, the haunted and undue fragrance of flowers that had filled the house for a while. But, when the food was in front of him he was hungry and ate. They all ate, even Aunt Emmy. Minnie did what waiting was necessary and did it, for once, without fluster. Jerry Pye seemed tired and subdued. Once Tom Carroll caught himself feeling sorry for him, once he tried to help him out in a story that was meant to be cheerful and fell flat.

"You know," said Minnie, in a flat voice, pouring coffee, "it seems as if Aunt Louise hadn't gone away so far as before it happened."

Tom Carroll knew what she meant. He felt it too—that presence of the dead, but not grimly nor as a ghost. The presence was as real as the October sky, and as removed from flesh. It did not have to mean that all tired souls were immortal—it had its own peace.

After the meal was over, Tom Carroll walked in the back yard and smoked with Jerry Pye. Now and then he remembered from childhood the fear that had walked there with him, with the scent of the overpowering flowers. But, search as he would, he could not find that fear. The few flowers left in the beds were bronze and scentless; there was no fear where they bloomed.

It was time to go in for the reading of Aunt Louise's will. Tom Carroll listened obediently. He did not even mention the names of Norman, Buckstone, and Carroll. Once, when Mr. Dabney, the lawyer, looked at him and said, "You are a member of the New York Bar, I believe, Mr. Carroll?" he felt surprised at being able to say "yes."

It was a long and personal will made up of many small bequests. He could see Aunt Louise going through her innumerable boxes, trying hard to be fair.

"To my nephew, Thomas Carroll, and his wife, Claire Fanshawe Carroll, the pair of silver candlesticks belonging to my dear Father."

Tom Carroll felt the slow red creeping into his face.

They shook hands with Mr. Dabney. They spoke of what was to be done. Tom Carroll did not proffer assistance. There was no need.

Jerry Pye was offering him a lift as far as Bradensburg—Minnie would be staying with Aunt Emmy for the next week or so, but he must get back to work. But Tom Carroll thought he had better wait till the morning.

"Well, I guess you'll be more comfortable here at that," said Jerry Pye. "I'll have to hit her up if I want to get home before 3 P.M. So long, Tom. You see Minnie doesn't step out with a handsomer fellow now the old man's away. And take care of the Pye candlesticks—at that, I guess they'll look better in your place than they would in ours. Our kids might use 'em for baseball bats. Say, give my best to Claire."

He was gone. "Now, Tommy," said Aunt Emmy in her tired,

indomitable voice, "you go back to the hotel and get a rest—you look tuckered out. Nelly Jervis is coming in here to get the supper. Half-past six."

They were sitting in the front parlor again that evening, he and she. It wasn't late, but Minnie had been sent to bed, unwilling. She wouldn't close an eye, she said; but they knew she was already asleep.

"It's queer what a good nurse Minnie is," said Aunt Emmy reflectively. "Seems as if it was the only thing that ever got her shut of her fussiness—taking care of sick people. You'd think she'd drop crumbs in the bed, but she never does. I don't know what we'd have done without her. Well, she's a right to be tired."

"How about you, Aunt Emmy?"

"Oh," said Aunt Emmy, "they used to say there'd be some people the Fool Killer would still be looking for on Judgment Day. I guess I'm one of them. Of course I'm tired, Tommy. When I'm tired enough, I'll tell you and go to bed."

"Look here, Aunt Emmy," said Tom Carroll, "if there's anything I can do—"

"And what could you do, Tommy?"

"Well, wouldn't you like a car?" he said, awkwardly, "or somebody to stay with you—or another place. They say those apartments over by the—"

"I was born here," said Aunt Emmy, with a snap of her lips, "and now Louise has gone, I've got just enough money to die here. It isn't the same, but I'm suited. And, of all the horrors of age, deliver me from a paid companion. If I need anything like that I'll get Susan Bache to move in here. She's a fool and she's a tattler," said Aunt Emmy, clearly, "but I'm used to her. And Minnie'll come up, every now and then. Don't worry about me, Tom Carroll. We've all of us been on your back long enough."

"On my back?" said Tom Carroll, astounded.

"Well, I'd like to know where else it was," said Aunt Emmy. "You got Louise's money back from that rascal that bamboozled her, and I know twice you pulled Jerry Pye out of the mudhole, and then there was Cousin Edna all those years. Not to speak of what you did for Melrose. Melrose was my own brother, but he ought to have been ashamed of himself, the way he hindered you. Oh, don't you worry about Waynesville, Tommy—you've no call. You did right to get out when you did and as you did, and Waynesville knows it, too. Not that Waynesville would ever admit George Washington was any great shakes, once he'd moved away. But you wait till you die, Tom Carroll"—and she actually chuckled—"and you see what the *Waynesville Blade* says about her distinguished son. They told Louise for twenty years she was crazy, teaching negroes to read and write. But they've got two columns about her this evening and an editorial. I've cut it out and I'm going to paste it under her picture. Louise was always the loving one, and I never grudged her that. But I did grudge her forgiving where I didn't see cause to forgive. But that's all done." She rustled the paper in her lap.

"How are your boys, Tommy?" she said. "They look smart enough in their pictures."

"We think they are," said Tom Carroll. "I hope you're right."

"They ought to be," said Aunt Emmy. "The Fanshawes never lacked smartness, whatever else they lacked, and your father was a bright man. Well, I've seen Jeremiah's and Minnie's. Boy and girl. Don't laugh at me, because it doesn't seem possible, but Jeremiah makes a good father. I never could get on with children—you ought to know that if anyone does—but I think they'll amount to something. Well, it's time the family was getting some sense again."

"Aunt Emmy!" said Tom Carroll, protestingly.

"Was this a happy house?" said Aunt Emmy, fiercely. "For me it was—yes—because I grew up in it. And I always had Louise and I don't regret anything. But was it happy for your mother and you? You know it wasn't, and a good thing your father took her out of it, adventurer or no adventurer, and a bad thing she had to come back. Well, we did our duty according to our lights. But that wasn't enough. There's no real reason, you know, why families have to get that way, except they seem to. But they will get to thinking they're God Almighty, and, after a while, that gets taken notice of. I'll say this—it wasn't the money with us. We held up our heads with it or without it. But maybe we held them too stiff."

She sank into a brooding silence. Behind her in the corner the vague shadows of innumerable Pyes and Merritts seemed to gather and mingle and wait. After a while she roused herself.

"Where are you going to live, Tommy?" she said.

"I've been thinking about a place in the country sometime," said Tom Carroll. "If Waynesville were a little different—"

Aunt Emmy shook her head.

"You couldn't come back here, Tommy," she said. "It's finished here. And that's just as well. But, if you're going to build your own house, you'd better do it soon. You won't be happy without it—you've got too much Merritt in you. The Merritts made their own places. It was the Pyes that sat on the eggs till finally they tried to hatch chickens out of a doorknob, because it was easier than looking for a new roost. But you haven't much Pye. All the same, you won't be contented till you've got some roots put down. The Fanshawes, they could live in a wagon and like it, but the Bouverins were like the Merritts—when they'd rambled enough, they cleared ground. And Claire looks a lot more Bouverin than Fanshawe to me, whether she likes it or not."

"I didn't know you knew Claire's family," said Tom Carroll.

"She probably wouldn't tell you," said Aunt Emmy. "Well, that's natural enough. Good Goshen! I remember Claire Fanshawe, a peaked little slip of a child, at Anna Bouverin's funeral, just before they left Bradensburg. The coffin was still open, and some ignoramus or other thought it would be fitting for all the grandchildren to come and kiss their grandma good-by. Mind you, after they'd said good-by to her once already, before she died. I could have told them better, little as I know children. Well, it didn't make much difference to Hattie; she always had the nerves of an ox. But Claire was just over typhoid and after they made her do it she had what *I'd* call a shaking chill, in a grown person. And *yet*, they made her get up and recite the Twenty-Third Psalm in front of everybody—just because she was smart for her age, and a little child shall lead them. Her mother didn't stop them—too proud of her knowing it, I guess. But that was the Fanshawe of it—they had to play-act whatever happened."

Tom Carroll had his head in his hands.

"She never told me," he said. "She never told me at all."

"No?" said Aunt Emmy, looking at him sharply. "Well, she was young and maybe she forgot it. I imagine Hattie did."

"Claire never has," said Tom Carroll.

"Well," said Aunt Emmy, "I'll tell you something, Tommy. When you get to my age you've seen life and death. And there's just one thing about death, once you start running away from the thought of it, it runs after you. Till finally you're scared even to talk about it and, even if your best friend dies, you'll forget him as quick as you can because the thought's always waiting. But once you can make yourself turn around and look at it—it's different. Oh, you can't help the grief. But you can get a child so it isn't afraid of the dark—though if you scared it first it'll take a longer while."

"Tell me," said Tom Carroll in a low voice, "were there—very sweet flowers—when my mother died?"

"It was just before Easter," said Aunt Emmy softly. "You could smell the flowers all through the house. But we didn't have any play-acting," she added, quickly. "Not with you. Melrose had that bee in his bonnet, but Louise put her foot down. But it's hard to explain to a child."

"It's hard to explain anyway," said Tom Carroll.

"That's true," said Aunt Emmy. "It's a queer thing," she said. "I never smell lilac without thinking of Lucy Marshall. She was a friend of mine, and then we fell out, and when we were young we used to play by a lilac bush in her yard. It used to trouble me for a long time before I put the two things together. But the pain went out of it then."

"Yes. The pain goes out when you know," said Tom Carroll. "It's not knowing that makes you afraid."

"If Hattie was closer to her, she could do it," said Aunt Emmy. "But the way things are—"

"It'll have to be me," said Tom Carroll. "And I don't know how."

"Well, you're fond of her," said Aunt Emmy. "They say that helps." She rose. "I'll give you the candlesticks in the morning, Tom."

"Can't I leave them with you, Aunt Emmy?"

"What's the use?" said Aunt Emmy practically. "To tell you the truth, Tommy, I'd got right tired of shining them. Besides, they'll look well in your house, when you get your house."

Too Early Spring

(1933)

I'M WRITING THIS DOWN because I don't ever want to forget the way it was. It doesn't seem as if I could, now, but they all tell you things change. And I guess they're right. Older people must have forgotten or they couldn't be the way they are. And that goes for even the best ones, like Dad and Mr. Grant. They try to understand but they don't seem to know how. And the others make you feel dirty or else they make you feel like a goof. Till, pretty soon, you begin to forget yourself—you begin to think, "Well, maybe they're right and it was that way." And that's the end of everything. So I've got to write this down. Because they smashed it forever but it wasn't the way they said.

Mr. Grant always says in comp. class: "Begin at the beginning." Only I don't know quite where the beginning was. We had a good summer at Big Lake but it was just the same summer. I worked pretty hard at the practice basket I rigged up in the barn, and I learned how to do the back jackknife. I'll never dive like Kerry but you want to be as all-around as you can. And, when I took my measurements, at the end of the summer, I was 5 ft. 9¾ and I'd gained 12 lbs. 6 oz. That isn't bad for going on sixteen and the old chest expansion was O.K. You don't want to get too heavy, because basketball's a fast game, but the year before was the year when I got my height, and I was so skinny, I got tired. But this year, Kerry helped me practice, a couple of times, and he seemed to think I had a good chance for the team. So I felt pretty set up—they'd never had a Sophomore on it before. And Kerry's a natural athlete, so that means a lot from him. He's a pretty good brother too. Most Juniors at State wouldn't bother with a fellow in High.

It sounds as if I were trying to run away from what I have to write down, but I'm not. I want to remember that summer, too, because it's the last happy one I'll ever have. Oh, when I'm an old man—thirty or forty—things may be all right again. But that's a long time to wait and it won't be the same.

And yet, that summer was different, too, in a way. So it must have started then, though I didn't know it. I went around with the gang as usual and we had a good time. But, every now and then, it would strike me we were acting like awful kids. They thought I was getting the big head, but I wasn't. It just wasn't much fun—even going to the cave. It was like going on shooting marbles when you're in High.

I had sense enough not to try to tag after Kerry and his crowd. You can't do that. But when they all got out on the lake in canoes, warm evenings, and somebody brought a phonograph along, I used to go down to the Point, all by myself, and listen and listen. Maybe they'd be talking or maybe they'd be singing, but it all sounded mysterious across the water. I wasn't trying to hear what they said, you know. That's the kind of thing Tot Pickens does. I'd just listen, with my arms around my knees—and somehow it would hurt me to listen—and yet I'd rather do that than be with the gang.

I was sitting under the four pines, one night, right down by the edge of the water. There was a big moon and they were singing. It's funny how you can be unhappy and nobody know it but yourself.

I was thinking about Sheila Coe. She's Kerry's girl. They

fight but they get along. She's awfully pretty and she can swim like a fool. Once Kerry sent me over with her tennis racket and we had quite a conversation. She was fine. And she didn't pull any of this big sister stuff, either, the way some girls will with a fellow's kid brother.

And when the canoe came along, by the edge of the lake, I thought for a moment it was her. I thought maybe she was looking for Kerry and maybe she'd stop and maybe she'd feel like talking to me again. I don't know why I thought that—I didn't have any reason. Then I saw it was just the Sharon kid, with a new kind of bob that made her look grown-up, and I felt sore. She didn't have any business out on the lake at her age. She was just a Sophomore in High, the same as me.

I chunked a stone in the water and it splashed right by the canoe, but she didn't squeal. She just said, "Fish," and chuckled. It struck me it was a kid's trick, trying to scare a kid.

"Hello, Helen," I said. "Where did you swipe the gunboat?"

"They don't know I've got it," she said. "Oh, hello, Chuck Peters. How's Big Lake?"

"All right," I said. "How was camp?"

"It was peachy," she said. "We had a peachy counselor, Miss Morgan. She was on the Wellesley field-hockey team."

"Well," I said, "we missed your society." Of course we hadn't, because they're across the lake and don't swim at our raft. But you ought to be polite.

"Thanks," she said. "Did you do the special reading for English? I thought it was dumb."

"It's always dumb," I said. "What canoe is that?"

"It's the old one," she said. "I'm not supposed to have it out at night. But you won't tell anybody, will you?"

"Be your age," I said. I felt generous. "I'll paddle a while, if you want," I said.

"All right," she said, so she brought it in and I got aboard. She went back in the bow and I took the paddle. I'm not strong on carting kids around, as a rule. But it was better than sitting there by myself.

"Where do you want to go?" I said.

"Oh, back towards the house," she said in a shy kind of voice. "I ought to, really. I just wanted to hear the singing."

"K.O.," I said. I didn't paddle fast, just let her slip. There was a lot of moon on the water. We kept around the edge so they wouldn't notice us. The singing sounded as if it came from a different country, a long way off.

She was a sensible kid, she didn't ask fool questions or giggle about nothing at all. Even when we went by Petters' Cove. That's where the lads from the bungalow colony go and it's pretty well populated on a warm night. You can hear them talking in low voices and now and then a laugh. Once Tot Pickens and a gang went over there with a flashlight, and a big Bohunk chased them for half a mile,

I felt funny, going by there with her. But I said, "Well, it's certainly Old Home Week"—in an offhand tone, because, after all, you've got to be sophisticated. And she said, "People are funny," in just the right sort of way. I took quite a shine to her after that and we talked. The Sharons have only been in town three years and somehow I'd never really noticed her before. Mrs. Sharon's awfully good-looking but she and Mr. Sharon fight. That's hard on a kid. And she was a quiet kid. She had a small kind of face and her eyes were sort of like a kitten's. You could see she got a great kick out of pretending to be grown-up—and yet it wasn't all pretending. A couple of times, I felt just as if I were talking to Sheila Coe. Only more comfortable, because, after all, we were the same age.

Do you know, after we put the canoe up, I walked all the way back home, around the lake? And most of the way, I ran. I felt swell too. I felt as if I could run forever and not stop. It was like finding something. I hadn't imagined anybody could ever feel the way I did about some things. And here was another person, even if it was a girl.

Kerry's door was open when I went by and he stuck his head out, and grinned.

"Well, kid," he said. Stepping out?"

"Sure. With Greta Garbo," I said, and grinned back to show I didn't mean it. I felt sort of lightheaded, with the run and everything.

"Look here, kid—" he said, as if he was going to say something. Then he stopped. But there was a funny look on his face.

And yet I didn't see her again till we were both back in High. Mr. Sharon's uncle died, back East, and they closed the cottage suddenly. But all the rest of the time at Big Lake, I kept remembering that night and her little face. If I'd seen her in daylight, first, it might have been different. No, it wouldn't have been.

All the same, I wasn't even thinking of her when we bumped into each other, the first day of school. It was raining and she had on a green slicker and her hair was curly under her hat. We grinned and said hello and had to run. But something happened to us, I guess.

I'll say this now—it wasn't like Tot Pickens and Mabel Palmer. It wasn't like Junior David and Betty Page—though they've been going together ever since kindergarten. It wasn't like any of those things. We didn't get sticky and sloppy. It wasn't like going with a girl.

Gosh, there'd be days and days when we'd hardly see each other, except in class. I had basketball practice almost every afternoon and sometimes evenings and she was taking music lessons four times a week. But you don't have to be always twos-ing with a person, if you feel that way about them. You seem to know the way they're thinking and feeling, the way you know yourself.

Now let me describe her. She had that little face and the eyes like a kitten's. When it rained, her hair curled all over the back of her neck. Her hair was yellow. She wasn't a tall girl but she wasn't chunky—just light and well made and quick. She was awfully alive without being nervous—she never bit her fingernails or chewed the end of her pencil, but she'd answer quicker than anyone in the class. Nearly everybody liked her, but she wasn't best friends with any particular girl, the mushy way they get. The teachers all thought a lot of her, even Miss Eagles. Well, I had to spoil that.

If we'd been like Tot and Mabel, we could have had a lot more time together, I guess. But Helen isn't a liar and I'm not a snake. It wasn't easy, going over to her house, because Mr. and Mrs. Sharon would be polite to each other in front of you and yet there'd be something wrong. And she'd have to be fair to both of them and they were always pulling at her. But we'd look at each other across the table and then it would be all right.

I don't know when it was that we knew we'd get married to each other, some time. We just started talking about it, one day, as if we always had. We were sensible, we knew it couldn't happen right off. We thought maybe when we were eighteen. That was two years but we knew we had to be educated. You don't get as good a job, if you aren't. Or that's what people say.

We weren't mushy either, like some people. We got to kissing each other good-by, sometimes, because that's what you do when you're in love. It was cool, the way she kissed you, it was like leaves. But lots of the time we wouldn't even talk about getting married, we'd just play checkers or go over the old Latin, or once in a while go to the movies with the gang. It was really a wonderful winter. I played every game after the first one and she'd sit in the gallery and watch and I'd know she was there. You could see her little green hat or her yellow hair. Those are the class colors, green and gold.

And it's a queer thing, but everybody seemed to be pleased. That's what I can't get over. They liked to see us together. The grown people, I mean. Oh, of course, we got kidded too. And old Mrs. Withers would ask me about "my little sweetheart," in that awful damp voice of hers. But, mostly, they were all right. Even Mother was all right, though she didn't like Mrs. Sharon. I did hear her say to Father, once, "Really, George, how long is this going to last? Sometimes I feel as if I just couldn't stand it."

Then Father chuckled and said to her, "Now, Mary, last year you were worried about him because he didn't take any interest in girls at all."

"Well," she said, "he still doesn't. Oh, Helen's a nice child— no credit to Eva Sharon—and thank heaven she doesn't giggle. Well, Charles is mature for *his* age too. But he acts so solemn about her. It isn't natural."

"Oh, let Charlie alone," said Father. "The boy's all right. He's just got a one-track mind."

But it wasn't so nice for us after the spring came.

In our part of the state, it comes pretty late, as a rule. But it was early this year. The little kids were out with scooters when usually they'd still be having snowfights and, all of a sudden, the radiators in the classrooms smelt dry. You'd got used to that smell for months—and then, there was a day when you hated it again and everybody kept asking to open the windows. The monitors had a tough time, that first week—they always do when spring starts—but this year it was worse than ever because it came when you didn't expect it.

Usually, basketball's over by the time spring really breaks, but this year it hit us while we still had three games to play. And it certainly played hell with us as a team. After Bladesburg nearly licked us, Mr. Grant called off all practice till the day before the St. Matthew's game. He knew we were stale—and they've been state champions two years. They'd have walked all over us, the way we were going.

The first thing I did was telephone Helen. Because that meant there were six extra afternoons we could have, if she could get rid of her music lessons any way. Well, she said, wasn't it wonderful, her music teacher had a cold? And that seemed just like Fate.

Well, that was a great week and we were so happy. We went to the movies five times and once Mrs. Sharon let us take her little car. She knew I didn't have a driving license but of course I've driven ever since I was thirteen and she said it was all right. She was funny—sometimes she'd be awfully kind and friendly to you and sometimes she'd be like a piece of dry ice. She was that way with Mr. Sharon too. But it was a wonderful ride. We got stuff out of the kitchen—the cook's awfully sold on Helen—and drove way out in the country. And we found an old house, with the windows gone, on top of a hill, and parked the car and took the stuff up to the house and ate it there. There weren't any chairs or tables but we pretended there were.

We pretended it was our house, after we were married. I'll never forget that. She'd even brought paper napkins and paper plates and she set two places on the floor.

"Well, Charles," she said, sitting opposite me, with her feet tucked under, "I don't suppose you remember the days we were both in school."

"Sure," I said—she was always much quicker pretending things than I was—"I remember them all right. That was before Tot Pickens got to be President." And we both laughed.

"It seems very distant in the past to me—we've been married so long," she said, as if she really believed it. She looked at me.

"Would you mind turning off the radio, dear?" she said. "This modern music always gets on my nerves."

"Have we got a radio?" I said.

"Of course, Chuck."

"With television?"

"Of course, Chuck."

"Gee, I'm glad," I said. I went and turned it off.

"Of course, if you *want* to listen to the late market reports—" she said just like Mrs. Sharon.

"Nope," I said. "The market—uh—closed firm today. Up twenty-six points."

"That's quite a long way up, isn't it?"

"Well, the country's perfectly sound at heart, in spite of this damnfool Congress," I said, like Father.

She lowered her eyes a minute, just like her mother, and pushed away her plate.

"I'm not very hungry tonight," .she said. "You won't mind if I go upstairs?"

"Aw, don't be like that," I said. It was too much like her mother.

"I was just seeing if I could," she said. "But I never will, Chuck."

"I'll never tell you you're nervous, either," I said. "I—oh, gosh!"

She grinned and it was all right. "Mr. Ashland and I have never had a serious dispute in our wedded lives," she said—and everybody knows who runs *that* family. "We just talk things over calmly and reach a satisfactory conclusion, usually mine."

"Say, what kind of house have we got?"

"It's a lovely house," she said. "We've got radios in every room and lots of servants. We've got a regular movie projector and a library full of good classics and there's always something in the icebox. I've got a shoe closet."

"A what?"

"A shoe closet. All my shoes are on tipped shelves, like Mother's. And all my dresses are on those padded hangers. And I say to the maid, 'Elsie, Madam will wear the new French model today.'"

"What are my clothes on?" I said. "Christmas trees?"

"Well," she said. "You've got lots of clothes and dogs. You smell of pipes and the open and something called Harrisburg tweed."

"I do not," I said. "I wish I had a dog. It's a long time since Jack."

"Oh, Chuck, I'm sorry," she said.

"Oh, that's all right," I said. "He was getting old and his ear was always bothering him. But he was a good pooch. Go ahead."

"Well," she said, "of course we give parties—"

"Cut the parties," I said.

"Chuck! They're grand ones!"

"I'm a homebody," I said. "Give me—er—my wife and my little family and—say, how many kids have we got, anyway?"

She counted on her fingers. "Seven."

"Good Lord," I said.

"Well, I always wanted seven. You can make it three, if you like."

"Oh, seven's all right, I suppose," I said. "But don't they get awfully in the way?"

"No," she said. "We have governesses and tutors and send them to boarding school."

"O.K.," I said. "But it's a strain on the old man's pocket-book,

just the same."

"Chuck, will you ever talk like that? Chuck, this is when we're rich." Then suddenly, she looked sad. "Oh, Chuck, do you suppose we ever will?" she said.

"Why, sure," I said.

"I wouldn't mind if it was only a dump," she said. "I could cook for you. I keep asking Hilda how she makes things."

I felt awfully funny. I felt as if I were going to cry.

"We'll do it," I said. "Don't you worry."

"Oh, Chuck, you're a comfort," she said.

I held her for a while. It was like holding something awfully precious. It wasn't mushy or that way. I know what that's like too.

"It takes so long to get old," she said. "I wish I could grow up tomorrow. I wish we both could."

"Don't you worry," I said. "It's going to be all right."

We didn't say much, going back in the car, but we were happy enough. I thought we passed Miss Eagles at the turn. That worried me a little because of the driving license. But, after all, Mrs. Sharon had said we could take the car.

We wanted to go back again, after that, but it was too far to walk and that was the only time we had the car. Mrs. Sharon was awfully nice about it but she said, thinking it over, maybe we'd better wait till I got a license. Well, Father didn't want me to get one till I was seventeen but I thought he might come around. I didn't want to do anything that would get Helen in a jam with her family. That shows how careful I was of her. Or thought I was.

All the same, we decided we'd do something to celebrate if the team won the St. Matthew's game. We thought it would be fun if we could get a steak and cook supper out somewhere—something like that. Of course we could have done it easily enough with a gang, but we didn't want a gang. We wanted to be alone together, the way we'd been at the house. That was all we wanted. I don't see what's wrong about that. We even took home the paper plates, so as not to litter things up.

Boy, that was a game! We beat them 36-34 and it took an extra period and I thought it would never end. That two-goal lead they had looked as big as the Rocky Mountains all the first half. And they gave me the full school cheer with nine Peters when we tied them up. You don't forget things like that.

Afterwards, Mr. Grant had a kind of spread for the team at his house and a lot of people came in. Kerry had driven down from State to see the game and that made me feel pretty swell. And what made me feel better yet was his taking me aside and saying, "Listen, kid, I don't want you to get the swelled head, but you did a good job. Well, just remember this. Don't let anybody kid you out of going to State. You'll like it up there." And Mr. Grant heard him and laughed and said, "Well, Peters, I'm not proselytizing. But your brother might think about some of the Eastern colleges." It was all like the kind of dream you have when you can do anything. It was wonderful.

Only Helen wasn't there because the only girls were older girls. I'd seen her for a minute, right after the game, and she was fine, but it was only a minute. I wanted to tell her about that big St. Matthew's forward and—oh, everything. Well, you like to talk things over with your girl.

Father and Mother were swell but they had to go on to some big shindy at the country club. And Kerry was going there with Sheila Coe. But Mr. Grant said he'd run me back to the house in his car and he did. He's a great guy. He made jokes about my being the infant phenomenon of basketball, and they were good jokes too. I didn't mind them. But, all the same, when I'd said good night to him and gone into the house, I felt sort of let down.

I knew I'd be tired the next day but I didn't feel sleepy yet. I was too excited. I wanted to talk to somebody. I wandered around downstairs and wondered if Ida was still up. Well, she wasn't, but she'd left half a chocolate cake, covered over, on the kitchen table, and a note on top of it, "Congratulations to Mister Charles Peters." Well, that was awfully nice of her and I ate some. Then I turned the radio on and got the time signal—eleven—and some snappy music. But still I didn't feel like hitting the hay.

So I thought I'd call up Helen and then I thought—probably she's asleep and Hilda or Mrs. Sharon will answer the phone and be sore. And then I thought—well, anyhow, I could go over and walk around the block and look at her house. I'd get some fresh air out of it, anyway, and it would be a little like seeing her.

So I did—and it was a swell night—cool and a lot of stars—and I felt like a king, walking over. All the lower part of the Sharon house was dark but a window upstairs was lit. I knew it was her window. I went around back of the driveway and whistled once—the whistle we made up. I never expected her to hear.

But she did, and there she was at the window, smiling. She made motions that she'd come down to the side door.

Honestly, it took my breath away when I saw her. She had on a kind of yellow thing over her night clothes and she looked so pretty. Her feet were so pretty in those slippers. You almost expected her to be carrying, one of those animals that kids like—she looked young enough. I know I oughtn't to have gone into the house. But we didn't think anything about it—we were just glad to see each other. We hadn't had any sort of chance to talk over the game.

We sat in front of the fire in the living room and she went out to the kitchen and got us cookies and milk. I wasn't really hungry, but it was like that time at the house, eating with her. Mr. and Mrs. Sharon were at the country club, too, so we weren't disturbing them or anything. We turned off the lights because there was plenty of light from the fire and Mr. Sharon's one of those people who can't stand having extra lights burning. Dad's that way about saving string.

It was quiet and lovely and the firelight made shadows on the ceiling. We talked a lot and then we just sat, each of us knowing the other was there. And the room got quieter and quieter and I'd told her about the game and I didn't feel excited or jumpy any more—just rested and happy. And then I knew by her breathing that she was asleep and I put my arm around her for just a minute. Because it was wonderful to hear that quiet breathing and know it was hers. I was going to wake her in a minute. I didn't realize how tired I was myself.

And then we were back in that house in the country and it was our home and we ought to have been happy. But something was wrong because there still wasn't any glass in the windows and a wind kept blowing through them and we tried to shut the doors but they wouldn't shut. It drove Helen distracted and we were both running through the house, trying to shut the doors, and we were cold and afraid. Then the sun rose outside the windows, burning and yellow and so big it covered the sky. And with the sun was a horrible, weeping voice. It was Mrs. Sharon's saying, "Oh, my God, oh my God."

I didn't know what had happened, for a minute, when I woke. And then I did and it was awful. Mrs. Sharon was saying "Oh, Helen—I trusted you…" and looking as if she were going to faint. And Mr. Sharon looked at her for a minute and his face was horrible and he said, "Bred in the bone," and she looked as if he'd hit her. Then he said to Helen—

I don't want to think of what they said. I don't want to think of any of the things they said. Mr. Sharon is a bad man. And she is a bad woman, even if she is Helen's mother. All the same, I could stand the things he said better than hers.

I don't want to think of any of it. And it is all spoiled now. Everything is spoiled. Miss Eagles saw us going to that house in the country and she said horrible things. They made Helen sick and she hasn't been back at school. There isn't any way I can see her. And if I could, it would be spoiled. We'd be thinking about the things they said.

I don't know how many of the people know, at school. But Tot Pickens passed me a note. And, that afternoon, I caught him behind his house. I'd have broken his nose if they hadn't pulled me off. I meant to. Mother cried when she heard about it and Dad took me into his room and talked to me. He said you can't lick the whole town. But I will anybody like Tot Pickens. Dad and Mother have been all right. But they say things about Helen and that's almost worse. They're for me because I'm their son. But they don't understand.

I thought I could talk to Kerry but I can't. He was nice but he looked at me such a funny way. I don't know—sort of impressed. It wasn't the way I wanted him to look. But he's been decent. He comes down almost every weekend and we play catch in the yard.

You see, I just go to school and back now. They want me to go with the gang, the way I did, but I can't do that. Not after Tot. Of course my marks are a lot better because I've got more time to study now. But it's lucky I haven't got Miss Eagles though Dad made her apologize. I couldn't recite to her.

I think Mr. Grant knows because he asked me to his house once and we had a conversation. Not about that, though I was terribly afraid he would. He showed me a lot of his old college things and the gold football he wears on his watch chain. He's got a lot of interesting things.

Then we got talking, somehow, about history and things like that and how times had changed. Why, there were kings and queens who got married younger than Helen and me. Only now we lived longer and had a lot more to learn. So it couldn't happen now. "It's civilization," he said. "And all civilization's against nature. But I suppose we've got to have it. Only sometimes it isn't easy." Well somehow or other, that made me feel less lonely. Before that I'd been feeling that I was the only person on earth who'd ever felt that way.

I'm going to Colorado, this summer, to a ranch, and next year, I'll go East to school. Mr. Grant says he thinks I can make the basketball team, if I work hard enough, though it isn't as big a game in the East as it is with us. Well, I'd like to show them something. It would be some satisfaction. He says not to be too fresh at first, but I won't be that.

It's a boys' school and there aren't even women teachers. And, maybe, afterwards, I could be a professional basketball player or something, where you don't have to see women at all. Kerry says I'll get over that; but I won't. They all sound like Mrs. Sharon to me now, when they laugh.

They're going to send Helen to a convent—I found out that. Maybe they'll let me see her before she goes. But, if we do, it will be all wrong and in front of people and everybody pretending. I sort of wish they don't—though I want to, terribly. When her mother took her upstairs that night—she wasn't the same Helen. She looked at me as if she was afraid of me. And no matter what they do for us now, they can't fix that.

THE STORY ABOUT THE ANTEATER

(1928)

THE YOUNGER CHILD sat bolt upright, her bedclothes wrapped around her.

"If you're going down to look at them," she whispered accusingly, "I'm coming, too! And Alice'll catch you."

"She won't catch me." Her elder sister's voice was scornful. "She's out in the pantry, helping. With the man from Gray's."

"All the same, I'm coming. I want to see if it's ice cream in little molds or just the smashed kind with strawberries. And, if Alice won't catch you, she won't catch me."

"It'll be molds," said the other, from the depths of experience,

"Mother always has molds for the Whitehouses. And Mr. Whitehouse sort of clicks in his throat and talks about sweets to the sweet. You'd think he'd know that's dopey but he doesn't. And, anyhow, it isn't your turn."

"It never is my turn," mourned her junior, tugging at the bedclothes.

"All right," said the elder. "If you *want* to go! And make a noise. And then they hear us and somebody comes up—"

"Sometimes they bring you things, when they come up," said the younger dreamily. "The man with the pink face did. And he said I was a little angel."

"Was he dopey!" said her elder, blightingly, "and anyhow,

you were sick afterwards and you know what Mother said about it."

The younger child sighed, a long sigh of defeat and resignation.

"All right," she said. "But next time it *is* my turn. And you tell me if it's in molds." Her elder nodded as she stole out of the door.

At the first turn of the stairs, a small landing offered an excellent observation post, provided one could get there unperceived. Jennifer Sharp reached it soundlessly and, curling herself up into the smallest possible space, stared eagerly down and across into the dining room.

She couldn't see the whole table. But she saw at once that Mrs. Whitehouse had a thing like a silver beetle in her hair, that Colonel Crandall looked more like a police dog than ever, and that there were little silver baskets of pink and white mints. That meant that it was really a grand dinner. She made a special note of the ice cream for Joan.

Talk and laughter drifted up to her—strange phrases and incomprehensible jests from another world, to be remembered, puzzled over, and analyzed for meaning or the lack of it, when she and Joan were alone. She hugged her knees, she was having a good time. Pretty soon, Father would light the little blue flame under the mysterious glass machine that made the coffee. She liked to see him do that.

She looked at him now, appraisingly. Colonel Crandall had fought Germans in trenches and Mr. Whitehouse had a bank to keep his money in. But Father, on the whole, was nicer than either of them. She remembered, as if looking back across a vast plain, when Father and Mother had merely been Father and Mother—huge, natural phenomena, beloved but inexplicable as the weather—unique of their kind. Now she was older—she knew that other people's fathers and mothers were different. Even Joan knew that, though Joan was still a great deal of a baby. Jennifer felt very old and rather benevolent as she considered herself and her parents and the babyishness of Joan.

Mr. Whitehouse was talking, but Father wanted to talk, too—she knew that from the quick little gesture he made with his left hand. Now they all laughed and Father leaned forward.

"That reminds me," he was saying, "of one of our favorite stories—" How young and amused his face looked, suddenly!

His eldest daughter settled back in the shadow, a bored but tolerant smile on her lips. She knew what was coming.

When Terry Farrell and Roger Sharp fell in love, the war to end war was just over, bobbed hair was still an issue, the movies did not talk and women's clothes couldn't be crazier. It was also generally admitted that the younger generation was wild but probably sound at heart and that, as soon as we got a business-man in the White House, things were going to be all right.

As for Terry and Roger, they were both wild and sophisti-cated. They would have told you so. Terry had been kissed by several men at several dances and Roger could remember the cu-rious, grimy incident of the girl at Fort Worth. So that showed you. They were entirely emancipated and free. But they fell in love very simply and unexpectedly—and their marriage was go-ing to be like no other marriage, because they knew all the right answers to all the questions, and had no intention of submitting to the commonplaces of life. At first, in fact, they were going to form a free union—they had read of that, in popular books of the period. But, somehow or other, as soon as Roger started to call, both families began to get interested. They had no idea of paying the slightest attention to their families. But, when your family happens to comment favorably on the man or girl that you are in love with, that is a hard thing to fight. Before they knew it, they were formally engaged, and liking it on the whole, though both of them agreed that a formal engagement was an outworn and ridiculous social custom.

They quarreled often enough, for they were young, and a trifle ferocious in the vehemence with which they expressed the views they knew to be right. These views had to do, in general, with freedom and personality, and were often supported by quotations from *The Golden Bough*. Neither of them had read *The Golden Bough* all the way through, but both agreed that it was a great book. But the quarrels were about generalities and had no sting. And always, before and after, was the sense of discovering in each other previously unsuspected but delightful potentialities and likenesses and beliefs.

As a matter of fact, they were quite a well-suited couple—"made for each other," as the saying used to go; though they would have hooted at the idea. They had read the minor works of Havelock Ellis and knew the name of Freud. They didn't believe in people being "made for each other"—they were too advanced.

It was ten days before the date set for their marriage that their first real quarrel occurred. And then, unfortunately, it didn't stop at generalities.

They had got away for the day from the presents and their families, to take a long walk in the country, with a picnic lunch. Both, in spite of themselves, were a little solemn, a little nervous. The atmosphere of Approaching Wedding weighed on them both—when their hands touched, the current ran, but, when they looked at each other, they felt strange. Terry had been shopping the day before—she was tired, she began to wish that Roger would not walk so fast. Roger was wondering if the sixth usher—the one who had been in the marines—would really turn up. His mind also held dark suspicions as to the probable behavior of the best man, when it came to such outworn customs as rice and shoes. They were sure that they were in love, sure now, that they wanted to be married. But their conversation was curiously polite.

The lunch did something for them, so did the peace of being alone. But they had forgotten the salt and Terry had rubbed her heel. When Roger got out his pipe, there was only tobacco left for half a smoke. Still, the wind was cool and the earth pleasant and, as they sat with their backs against a gray boulder in the middle of a green field, they began to think more naturally. The current between their linked hands ran stronger—in a moment or two, they would be the selves they had always known.

It was, perhaps, unfortunate that Roger should have selected that particular moment in which to tell the anteater story.

He knocked out his pipe and smiled, suddenly, at something in his mind. Terry felt a knock at her heart, a sudden sweetness on her tongue—how young and amused he always looked when he smiled! She smiled back at him, her whole face changing.

"What is it, darling?" she said.

He laughed. "Oh nothing," he said. "I just happened to remember. Did you ever hear the story about the anteater?"

She shook her head.

"Well," he began. "Oh, you must have heard it—sure you haven't? Well, anyway, there was a little town down South…

"And the coon said, 'Why, lady, that ain't no anteater—that's Edward!'" he finished, triumphantly, a few moments later. He couldn't help laughing when he had finished—the silly tale always amused him, old as it was. Then he looked at Terry and saw that she was not laughing.

"Why, what's the matter?" he said, mechanically. "Are you cold, dear, or—"

Her hand, which had been slowly stiffening in his clasp, now withdrew itself entirely from his.

"No," she said, staring ahead of her, "I'm all right. Thanks."

He looked at her. There was somebody there he had never seen before.

"Well," he said, confusedly, "well." Then his mouth set, his jaw stuck out, he also regarded the landscape.

Terry stole a glance at him. It was terrible and appalling to see him sitting there, looking bleak and estranged. She wanted to speak, to throw herself at him, to say: "Oh, it's all my fault— it's all my fault!" and know the luxury of saying it. Then she remembered the anteater and her heart hardened.

It was not even, she told herself sternly, as if it were a dirty story. It wasn't—and, if it had been, weren't they always going to be frank and emancipated with each other about things like that? But it was just the kind of story she'd always hated—cruel and—yes—vulgar. Not even healthily vulgar—vulgar with no redeeming adjective. He ought to have known she hated that kind of story. He ought to have known!

If love meant anything, according to the books, it meant understanding the other person, didn't it? And, if you didn't understand them, in such a little thing, why, what was life going to be afterwards? Love was like a new silver dollar—bright, untarnished and whole. There could be no possible compromises with love.

All these confused but vehement thoughts flashed through her mind. She also knew that she was tired and wind-blown and jumpy and that the rub on her heel was a little red spot of pain. And then Roger was speaking.

"I'm sorry you found my story so unamusing," he said in stiff tones of injury and accusation. "If I'd known about the way you felt, I'd have tried to tell a funnier one—even if we did say—"

He stopped, his frozen face turned toward her. She could feel the muscles of her own face tighten and freeze in answer.

"I wasn't in the *least* shocked, I assure you," she said in the same, stilted voice. "I just didn't think it was very funny. That's all."

"I get you. Well, pardon my glove," he said, and turned to the landscape.

A little pulse of anger began to beat in her wrist. Something was being hurt, something was being broken. If he'd only been Roger and kissed her instead of saying—well, it was his fault, now.

"No, I didn't think it was funny at all," she said, in a voice whose sharpness surprised her, "if you want to know. Just sort of cruel and common and—well, the poor Negro—"

"That's right!" he said, in a voice of bitter irritation, "pity the coon! Pity everybody but the person who's trying to amuse you! I think it's a damn funny story—always have—and—"

They were both on their feet and stabbing at each other, now.

"And it's vulgar," she was saying, hotly, "plain vulgar—not even dirty enough to be funny. Anteater indeed! Why, Roger Sharp, it's—"

"Where's that sense of humor you were always talking about?" he was shouting. "My God, what's happened to you, Terry? I always thought you were—and here you—"

"Well, we both of us certainly seem to have been mistaken about each other," she could hear her strange voice, saying. Then, even more dreadfully, came his unfamiliar accents, "Well, if that's the way you feel about it, we certainly have."

They looked at each other, aghast. "Here!" she was saying, "here! Oh, Lord, why won't it come off my finger?"

"You keep that on—do you hear, you damn little fool?" he

roared at her, so unexpectedly that she started, tripped, caught her shoe in a cleft of rock, fell awkwardly, and, in spite of all her resolves, burst undignifiedly and conventionally into a passion of tears.

Then there was the reconciliation. It took place, no doubt, on entirely conventional lines, and was studded with "No, it was my fault! Say it was!" but, to them it was an event unique in history.

Terry thought it over remorsefully, that evening, waiting for Roger. Roger was right. She had been a little fool. She knew the inexplicable solace of feeling that she had been a little fool.

And yet, they had said those things to each other, and meant them. He had hurt her, she had actually meant to hurt him. She stared at these facts, solemnly. Love, the bright silver dollar. Not like the commonplace coins in other people's pockets. But something special, different—already a little, ever-so-faintly tarnished, as a pane is tarnished by breath?

She had been a little fool. But she couldn't quite forget the anteater.

Then she was in Roger's arms—and knew, with utter confidence, that she and Roger were different. They were always going to be different. Their marriage wouldn't ever be like any other marriage in the world.

The Sharps had been married for exactly six years and five hours and Terry, looking across the table at the clever, intelligent face of her affectionate and satisfactory husband, suddenly found herself most desolately alone.

It had been a mistake in the first place—going to the Lattimores for dinner on their own anniversary. Mr. Lattimore was the head of Roger's company—Mrs. Lattimore's invitation had almost the force of a royal command. They had talked it over,

Roger and she, and decided, sensibly, that they couldn't get out of it. But, all the same, it had been a mistake.

They were rational, modern human beings, she assured herself ferociously. They weren't like the horrible married couples in the cartoons—the little woman asking her baffled mate if he remembered what date it was, and the rest of it. They thought better of life and love than to tie either of them to an artificial scheme of days. They were different. Nevertheless, there had been a time when they had said to each other, with foolish smiles, "We've been married a week—or a month—or a year! Just think of it!" This time now seemed to her, as she looked back on it coldly, a geologic age away.

She considered Roger with odd dispassionateness. Yes, there he was—an intelligent, rising young man in his first thirties. Not particularly handsome but indubitably attractive—charming, when he chose—a loyal friend, a good father, a husband one could take pride in. And it seemed to her that if he made that nervous little gesture with his left hand again—or told the anteater story—she would scream.

It was funny that the knowledge that you had lost everything that you had most counted upon should come to you at a formal dinner party, while you talked over the war days with a dark-haired officer whose voice had the honey of the South in it. Then she remembered that she and Roger had first discovered their love for each other, not upon a moon-swept lawn, but in the fly-specked waiting room of a minor railroad station—and the present event began to seem less funny. Life was like that. It gave, unexpectedly, abruptly, with no regard for stage setting or the properties of romance. And, as unexpectedly and abruptly, it took away.

While her mouth went on talking, a part of her mind searched numbly and painfully for the reasons which had brought this calamity about. They had loved each other in the beginning—even now, she was sure of that. They had tried to be wise, they had not broken faith, they had been frank and gay. No deep division of nature sundered them—no innate fault in either, spreading under pressure, to break the walls of their house apart. She looked for a guilty party but she could find none. There was only a progression of days; a succession of tiny events that followed in each other's footsteps without haste or rest. That was all, but that seemed to have been enough. And Roger was looking over at her—with that same odd, exploring glance she had used a moment ago.

What remained? A house with a little boy asleep in it, a custom of life, certain habits, certain memories, certain hardships lived through together. Enough for most people, perhaps? They had wanted more than that. Something said to her, "Well and if—after all—the real thing hasn't even come?" She turned to her dinner partner, for the first time really seeing him. When you did see him, he was quite a charming person. His voice was delightful. There was nothing in him in the least like Roger Sharp.

She laughed and saw, at the laugh, something wake in his eyes. He, too, had not been really conscious of her, before. But he was, now. She was not thirty, yet—she had kept her looks. She felt old powers, old states of mind flow back to her; things she had thought forgotten, the glamor of first youth. Somewhere, on the curve of a dark lake, a boat was drifting—a man was talking to her—she could not see his face but she knew it was not Roger's—

She was roused from her waking dream by Mrs. Lattimore's voice.

"Why, I'd never have dreamt!" Mrs. Lattimore was saying, "I had no idea!" She called down the table, "George! Do you know it's these people's anniversary—so sweet of them to come—and I positively had to worm it out of Mr. Sharp!"

Terry went hot and cold all over. She was sensible, she was brokenhearted, love was a myth, but she had particularly depended on Roger not to tell anybody that this was their anniversary. And Roger had told.

She lived through the congratulations and the customary jokes about "Well, this is your seventh year beginning—and you know what they say about the seventh year!" She even lived through Mrs. Lattimore's pensive "Six years! Why, my dear, I never would have believed it! You're children—positive children!"

She could have bitten Mrs. Lattimore. "Children!" she thought, indignantly, "When I—when we—when everything's in ruins!" She "tried to freeze Roger, at long distance, but he was not looking her way. And then she caught her breath, for a worse fate was in store for her.

Someone, most unhappily, had brought up the subject of pet animals. She saw a light break slowly on Roger's face—she saw him lean forward. She prayed for the roof to fall, for time to stop, for Mrs. Lattimore to explode like a Roman candle into green and purple stars. But, even as she prayed, she knew that it was no use. Roger was going to tell the anteater story.

The story no longer seemed shocking to her, or even cruel. But it epitomized all the years of her life with Roger. In the course of those years, she calculated desperately, she had heard that story at least a hundred times.

Somehow—she never knew how—she managed to survive the hundred-and-first recital, from the hideously familiar, "Well, there was a little town down South..." to the jubilant "That's Edward!" at the end. She even summoned up a fixed smile to meet the tempest of laughter that followed. And then, mercifully, Mrs. Lattimore was giving the signal to rise.

The men hung behind—the anteater story had been capped by another. Terry found herself, unexpectedly, tetè-à-tetè with Mrs. Lattimore.

"My dear," the great lady was saying, "I'd rather have asked you another night, of course, if I'd known. But I am very glad you could come tonight. George particularly wished Mr. Colden to meet your brilliant husband. They are going into that Western project together, you know, and Tom Colden leaves tomorrow. So we both appreciate your kindness in coming."

Terry found a sudden queer pulse of warmth through the cold fog that seemed to envelop her. "Oh," she stammered, "but Roger and I have been married for years—and we were delighted to come—" She looked at the older woman. "Tell me, though," she said, with an irrepressible burst of confidence, "doesn't it ever seem to you as if you couldn't bear to hear a certain story again—not if you *died?*"

A gleam of mirth appeared in Mrs. Lattimore's eyes.

"My dear," she said, "has George ever told you about his trip to Peru?"

"No."

"Well, don't let him." She reflected. "Or, no—do let him," she said. "Poor George—he does get such fun out of it. And you would be a new audience. But it happened fifteen years ago, my dear, and I think I could repeat every word after him verbatim, once he's started. Even so I often feel as if he'd never stop."

"And then what do you do?" said Terry, breathlessly—far too interested now to remember tact.

The older woman smiled. "I think of the story I am going to tell about the guide in the Uffizi gallery," she said. "George must have heard that story ten thousand times. But he's still alive."

She put her hand on the younger woman's arm.

"We're all of us alike, my dear," she said. "When I'm an old lady in a wheel chair, George will still be telling me about Peru. But then, if he didn't, I wouldn't know he was George."

She turned away, leaving Terry to ponder over the words. Her anger was not appeased—her life still lay about her in ruins. But, when the dark young officer came into the room, she noticed that his face seemed rather commonplace and his voice was merely a pleasant voice.

Mr. Colden's car dropped the Sharps at their house. The two men stayed at the gate for a moment, talking—Terry ran in to see after the boy. He was sleeping peacefully with his fists tight shut; he looked like Roger in his sleep. Suddenly, all around her were the familiar sights and sounds of home. She felt tired and as if she had come back from a long journey.

She went downstairs. Roger was just coming in. He looked tired, too, she noticed, but exultant as well.

"Colden had to run," he said at once. "Left good-by for you—hoped you wouldn't mind said awfully nice things. He's really a great old boy, Terry. And, as for this new Western business—"

He noticed the grave look on her face and his own grew grave.

"I *am* sorry, darling," he said. "Did you mind it a lot? Well, I did—but it couldn't be helped. You bet your life that next time—"

"Oh, next time—" she said, and kissed him. "Of course I didn't mind. We're different, aren't we?"

That intelligent matron, Mrs. Roger Sharp, now seated at the foot of her own dinner table, from time to time made the appropriate interjections—the "Really? "s and "Yes indeed"s and "That's what I always tell Roger"s—which comprised the whole duty of a hostess in Colonel Crandall's case. Colonel Crandall was singularly restful—give him these few crumbs and he could be depended upon to talk indefinitely and yet without creating a conversational desert around him. Mrs. Sharp was very grateful to him at the moment. She wanted to retire to a secret place in her mind and observe her own dinner party, for an instant, as a spectator—and Colonel Crandall was giving her the chance.

It was going very well indeed. She had hoped for it from the first, but now she was sure of it and she gave a tiny, inaudible sigh of relief. Roger was at his best—the young Durwards had recovered from their initial shyness—Mr. Whitehouse had not yet started talking politics—the soufflé had been a success. She relaxed a little and let her mind drift off upon other things.

Tomorrow, Roger must remember about the light gray suit, she must make a dental appointment for Jennifer, Mrs. Quaritch must be dealt with tactfully in the matter of the committee. It was too early to decide about camp for the girls but Roger Junior must know they were proud of his marks, and if Mother intended to give up her trip just because of poor old Miss Tompkins—well, something would have to be done. There were also the questions of the new oil furnace, the School board and the Brewster wedding. But none of these really bothered her—her life was always busy—and, at the moment, she felt an unwonted desire to look back into Time.

Over twenty years since the Armistice. Twenty years. And Roger Junior was seventeen—and she and Roger had been married since nineteen-twenty. Pretty soon they would be celebrating their twentieth anniversary. It seemed incredible but it was true.

She looked back through those years, seeing an ever-younger creature with her own face, a creature that laughed or wept for forgotten reasons, ran wildly here, sat solemn as a young judge there. She felt a pang of sympathy for that young heedlessness, a pang of humor as well. She was not old but she had been so very young.

Roger and she—the beginning—the first years—Roger Junior's birth. The house on Edgehill Road, the one with the plate rail in the dining room, and crying when they left because they'd never be so happy again, but they had, and it was an inconvenient house. Being jealous of Milly Baldwin—and how foolish!—and the awful country-club dance where Roger got drunk; and it wasn't awful any more. The queer, piled years of the boom—the crash—the bad time—Roger coming home after Tom Colden's suicide and the look on his face. Jennifer. Joan. Houses. People. Events. And always the headlines in the papers, the voices on the radio, dinning, dinning "No security—trouble—disaster—no security." And yet, out of insecurity, they had loved and made children. Out of insecurity, for the space of breath, for an hour, they had built, and now and then found peace.

No, there's no guarantee, she thought. There's no guarantee. When you're young, you think there is, but there isn't. And yet I'd do it over. Pretty soon we'll have been married twenty years.

"Yes, that's what I always tell Roger," she said, automatically. Colonel Crandall smiled and proceeded. He was still quite handsome, she thought, in his dark way, but he was getting very bald. Roger's hair had a few gray threads in it but it was still thick and unruly. She liked men to keep their hair. She remembered, a long while ago, thinking something or other about Colonel Crandall's voice, but she could not remember what she had thought.

She noticed a small white speck on the curve of the stairway but said nothing. The wrapper was warm and, if Jennifer wasn't noticed, she would creep back to bed soon enough. It was different with Joan.

Suddenly, she was alert. Mrs. Durward, at Roger's end of the table, had mentioned the Zoo. She knew what that meant—Zoo—the new buildings—the new Housing Commissioner—and Mr. Whitehouse let loose on his favorite political grievance all through the end of dinner. She caught Roger's eye for a miraculous instant. Mr. Whitehouse was already clearing his throat. But Roger had the signal. Roger would save them. She saw his left hand tapping in its little gesture—felt him suddenly draw the party together. How young and amused his face looked, under the candlelight!

"That reminds me of one of our favorite stories," he was saying. She sank back in her chair. A deep content pervaded her. He was going to tell the anteater story—and, even if some of the people had heard it, they would have to laugh, he always told it so well. She smiled in anticipation of the triumphant "That's Edward!" And, after that, if Mr. Whitehouse still threatened, she herself would tell the story about Joan and the watering pot.

Jennifer crept back into the darkened room.

"Well?" said an eager whisper from the other bed. Jennifer drew a long breath. The memory of the lighted dinner table rose before her, varicolored, glittering, portentous—a stately omen—a thing of splendor and mystery, to be pondered upon for days. How could she ever make Joan see it as she had seen it? And Joan was such a baby, anyway.

"Oh—nobody saw me," she said, in a bored voice. "But it was in molds, that's all—oh yes—and Father told the anteater story again."

SCHOONER FAIRCHILD'S CLASS
(1938)

WHEN HE SAID good night to his son and Tom Drury and the rest of them, Lane Parrington walked down the steps of the Leaf Club and stood, for a moment, breathing in the night air. He had made the speech they'd asked him to make, and taken pains with it, too—but now he was wondering whether it wasn't the same old graduate's speech after all. He hadn't meant it to be so, but you ran into a lingo, once you started putting thoughts on paper you began to view with alarm and talk about imperiled bulwarks and the American way of life.

And yet he'd been genuinely pleased when the invitation came—and they'd asked him three months ahead. That meant something, even to the Lane Parrington of United Investments— it was curious how old bonds held. He had been decorated by two foreign governments and had declined a ministry—there was the place in Virginia, the place on Long Island, the farm in Vermont and the big apartment on the river. There were the statements issued when sailing for Europe and the photographs and articles in news-weeklies and magazines. And yet he had been pleased when they asked him to speak at the annual dinner of an undergraduate club in his own college. Of course, the Leaf was a little different, as all Leaf members knew. When he had been a new member, as his son was now, the speech had been made by a Secretary of State.

Well, he'd done well enough, he supposed—at least Ted had come up, afterward, a little shyly, and said, "Well, Dad, you're quite an orator." But, once or twice, in the course of the speech, he had caught Ted fiddling with his coffee spoon. They were almost always too long—those speeches by graduates—he had tried to remember that. But he couldn't help running a little overtime—not after he'd got up and seen them waiting there. They were only boys, of course, but boys who would soon be men with men's responsibilities—he had even made a point of that.

One of the things about the Leaf—you got a chance of hearing what—well, what really important men thought of the state of the world and the state of the nation. They could get a lot from professors but hardly that. So, when a sensible fellow got up to explain what sensible men really thought about this business at Washington—why, damn it, nobody was going to ring a gong on him! And they'd clapped him well, at the end, and Ted's face had looked relieved. They always clapped well, at the end.

Afterward, he had rather hoped to meet Ted's friends and get in a little closer touch with them than he did at the place in Virginia or the place on Long Island or the apartment in New York. He saw them there, of course—they got in cars and out of cars, they dressed and went to dances, they played on the tennis courts and swam in the pool. They were a good crowd—a typical Leaf crowd, well-exercised and well-mannered. They were polite to Cora and polite to him. He offered them cigars now and then; during the last two years he offered them whisky and soda. They listened to what he had to say and, if he told a good story, they usually laughed at it. They played tennis with him, occasionally, and said, "Good shot, sir!"—afterward, they played harder tennis. One of them was Ted, his son, well-mannered, well-exercised, a member of the Leaf. He could talk to

Ted about college athletics, the college curriculum, his allowance, the weather, the virtues of capitalism and whether to get a new beach wagon this summer. Now, to these subjects was added the Leaf and the virtues of the Leaf. He could talk to Ted about any number of things.

Nevertheless, sometimes when the annual dinner was over, there would be a little group at the Leaf around this graduate or that. He remembered one such group his senior year, around a sharp-tongued old man with hooded eyes. The ex-senator was old and broken, but they'd stayed up till two while his caustic voice made hay of accepted catchwords. Well, he had met Ted's friends and remembered most of their names. They had congratulated him on his speech and he had drunk a highball with them. It had all been in accord with the best traditions of the Leaf but it hadn't lasted very long.

For a moment, indeed, he had almost gotten into an argument with one of them—the pink-faced, incredibly youthful one with the glasses who was head of the Student Union—they hadn't had student unions in his time. He had been answering a couple of questions quite informally, using slang, and the pink-faced youth had broken in with, "But, look here, sir—I mean, that was a good speech you made from the conservative point of view and all that—but when you talk about labor's being made responsible, just what do you mean and how far do you go? Do you mean you want to scrap the Wagner Act or amend it or what?"

But then the rest of them had said, "Oh, don't mind Stu—he's our communist. Skip it, Stu—how's dialectic materialism today?" and it had passed off in kidding. Lane Parrington felt a little sorry about that—he would have enjoyed a good argument with an intelligent youngster—he was certainly broad-minded enough for that. But, instead, he'd declined another highball and said, well, he supposed he ought to be getting back to the inn. It had all been very well-mannered and in accord with the best traditions of the Leaf. He wondered how the old ex-senator had got them to talk.

Ted had offered to walk along with him, of course, and, equally, of course, he had declined. Now he stood for a moment on the sidewalk, wondering whether he ought to look in at class headquarters before going back to the inn. He ought to, he supposed—after all, it was his thirtieth reunion. It would be full of cigar smoke and voices and there would be a drunk from another class—there was always, somehow or other, a drunk from another class who insisted on leading cheers. And Schooner Fairchild, the class funny man, would be telling stories—the one about the Kickapoo chief, the one about President Dodge and the telephone. As it was in the beginning, is now and ever shall be. He didn't dislike Schooner Fairchild any more—you couldn't dislike a man who had wasted his life. But Schooner, somehow, had never seemed conscious of that.

Yes, he'd go to class headquarters—he'd go, if for no other reason than to prove that he did not dislike Schooner Fairchild. He started walking down Club Row. There were twelve of the clubhouses now—there had been only eight in his time. They all looked very much alike, even the new ones—it took an initiated eye to detect the slight enormous differences—to know that Wampum, in spite of its pretentious lanterns, was second-rate and would always be second-rate, while Abbey, small and dingy, ranked with Momus and the Leaf. Parrington stood still, reliving the moment of more than thirty years ago when he'd gotten the bid from Wampum and thought he would have to accept it. It hadn't been necessary—the Leaf messenger had knocked on his door at just three minutes to nine. But whenever he passed the Wampum house he remembered. For almost an hour, it had seemed as if the destined career of Lane Parrington wasn't going to turn out right after all.

The small agonies of youth—they were unimportant, of course, but they left a mark. And he'd had to succeed—he'd had to have the Leaf, just as later on, he'd had to have money—he wasn't a Schooner Fairchild, to take things as they came. You were geared like that or you weren't—if you weren't, you might as well stay in Emmetsburg and end up as a harried high school principal with sick headaches and a fine Spencerian handwriting, as his father had. But he had wanted to get out of Emmetsburg the moment he had realized there were other places to go.

He remembered a look through a microscope and a lashing, tailed thing that swam. There were only two classes of people, the wigglers and the ones who stood still—he should have made his speech on that—it would have been a better speech. And the ones who stood still didn't like the wigglers—that, too, he knew, from experience. If they saw a wiggler coining, they closed ranks and opposed their large, well-mannered inertia to the brusque, ill-mannered life. Later on, of course, they gave in gracefully, but without real liking. He had made the Leaf on his record—and a very good record it had had to be. He had even spent three painful seasons with the track squad, just to demonstrate that desirable all-aroundness that was one of the talking points. And even so, they had smelled it—they had known, instinctively, that he wasn't quite their kind. Tom Drury, for instance, had always been pleasant enough—but Tom Drury had always made him feel that he was talking a little too much and a little too loud. Tom Drury, who, even then, had looked like a magnificent sheep. But he had also been class president, and the heir to Drury and Son. And yet, they all liked Schooner Fairchild—they liked him still.

And here was the end of Club Row, and the Momus House. He stopped and took out a cigar. It was silly to fight old battles, especially when they were won. If they asked the Drurys to dinner now, the Drurys came—he'd been offered and declined a partnership in Drury and Son. But he had helped Tom out with some of their affiliates and Tom had needed help—Tom would always be impressive, of course, but it took more than impressiveness to handle certain things. And now Ted was coming along—and Ted was sound as a bell. So sound he might marry one of the Drury daughters, if he wanted—though that was Ted's business. He wondered if he wanted Ted to marry young. He had done so himself—on the whole, it had been a mistake.

Funny, how things mixed in your mind. As always, when he remembered Dorothy, there was the sharp, sweet smell of her perfume; then the stubborn, competent look of her hands on the wheel of a car. They had been too much alike to have married—lucky they'd found it out in time. She had let him keep the child—of course he would have fought for it anyway—but it was considered very modern in those days. Then the war had washed over and obliterated a great deal—afterward, he had married Cora. And that had worked out as it should—Ted was fond of her and she treated him with just the right shade of companionableness. Most things worked out in the end. He wondered if Dorothy had gotten what she wanted at last—he supposed she had, with her Texan. But she'd died in a hospital at Galveston, ten years ago, trying to have the Texan's child, so he couldn't ask her now. They had warned her about having more children—but, as soon as you warned Dorothy about anything, that was what she wanted to do. He could have told them. But the Texan was one of those handsome, chivalrous men.

Strange, that out of their two warring ambitions should have come the sound, reliable, healthy Ted. But, no, it wasn't strange—he had planned it as carefully as one could, and Cora had helped a great deal. Cora never got out of her depth and she had a fine social sense. And the very best nurses and schools from the very first—and there you were! You did it as you ran a business—picked the right people and gave them authority. He had hardly ever had to interfere himself.

There would be a great deal of money—but that could be taken care of—there were ways. There were trust funds and foundations and clever secretaries. And Ted need never realize it. There was no reason he should—no reason in the least. Ted could think he was doing it all.

He pulled hard on his cigar and started to walk away. For the door of the Momus Club had suddenly swung open, emitting a gush of light and a small, chubby, gray-haired figure with a turned-up nose and a jack-o'-lantern grin. It stood on the steps for a moment, saying good night a dozen times and laughing. Lane Parrington walked fast but it was no use. He heard pattering footsteps behind him—a voice cried, "Ought-Eight!" with conviction, then, "Lane Parrington, b'gosh!" He stopped and turned.

"Oh, hello, Schooner," he said, unenthusiastically. "Your dinner over, too?"

"Oh, the boys'll keep it up till three," said Schooner Fairchild, mopping his pink brow. "But, after an hour and a half, I told them it was time they got some other poor devil at the piano. I'm not as young as I was." He panted, comically, and linked arms with Lane Parrington. "Class headquarters?" he said. "I shouldn't go—Minnie will scalp me. But I will."

"Well," said Lane Parrington uncomfortably—he hated having his arm held, "I suppose we ought to look in."

"Duty, Mr. Easy, always duty," said Schooner Fairchild and chuckled. "Hey, don't walk so fast—an old man can't keep up with you." He stopped and mopped his brow again. "By the way," he said, "that's a fine boy of yours, Lane."

"Oh," said Lane Parrington awkwardly. "Thanks. But I didn't know—"

"Saw something of him last summer," said Schooner Fairchild cheerfully. "Sylvia brought him around to the house. He could have a rather nice baritone, if he wanted."

"Baritone?" said Lane Parrington. "Sylvia?"

"Eldest daughter and pride of the Fairchild chateau," said Schooner Fairchild, slurring his words by a tiny fraction. "She collects 'em —not always—always with Father's approval. But your boy's a nice boy. Serious, of course." He chuckled again, it seemed to Lane Parrington maddeningly. "Oh, the sailor said to the admiral, and the admiral said he—" he chanted. "Remember that one, Lane?"

"No," said Lane Parrington.

"That's right," said Schooner Fairchild, amiably. "Stupid of me. I thought for a minute, you'd been in the quartet. But that was dear old Pozzy Banks. Poor Pozzy—he never could sing 'The Last Rose of Summer' properly till he was as drunk as an owl. A man of great talents. I hoped he'd be here this time but he couldn't make it. He wanted to come," he hummed, "but he didn't have the fare..."

"That's too bad," said Lane Parrington, seriously. "And yet, with business picking up..."

Schooner Fairchild looked at him queerly, for an instant. "Oh, bless you!" he said. "Pozzy never had a nickel. But he was fun." He tugged at Lane Parrington's arm, as they turned a corner and saw an electric sign—1908—above the door. "Well, here we go!" he said.

An hour later, Lane Parrington decided that it was just as he had expected. True, the drunk from the unidentified class had gone home. But others, from other classes, had arrived. And Schooner Fairchild was sitting at the piano.

He himself was wedged uncomfortably at the back of the room between Ed Runner and a man whose name, he thought, was either Ferguson or Whitelaw, but who, in any case, addressed him as "Lane, old boy." This made conversation difficult, for it was hard to call his neighbor either "Fergy" or "Whitey" without being sure of his name. On the other hand, conversation with Ed Runner was equally difficult, for that gentleman had embarked upon an interminable reminiscence whose point turned upon the exact location of Bill Webley's room Sophomore year. As Lane Parrington had never been in any of Bill Webley's rooms, he had very little to add to the discussion. He was also drinking beer, which never agreed with him, and the cigar smoke stung his eyes. And around the singer and the piano boiled and seethed a motley crew of graduates of all classes—the Roman togas of 1913, the convict stripes of 1935, the shorts and explorers' helmets of 1928. For the news had somehow gone around, through the various class headquarters, that Schooner Fairchild was doing his stuff—and, here and there, among the crowd, were undergraduates, who had heard from brothers and uncles about Schooner Fairchild, but had never seen him before in the flesh.

He had told the story of the Kickapoo chief, he had given the imitation of President Dodge and the telephone. Both these and other efforts, Lane Parrington noted wonderingly, had been received with tumultuous cheers. Now he played a few chords and swung around on the piano stool.

"I shall now," he said, with his cherubic face very solemn, "emit my positively last and final number—an imitation of dear old Pozzy Banks, attempting to sing 'The Last Rose of Summer' while under the influence of wine. Not all of you have been privileged to know dear old Pozzy—a man of the most varied and diverse talents—it is our great regret that he is not with us tonight. But for those of you who were not privileged to know

Pozzy, may I state as an introduction that dear old Pozzy is built something on the lines of a truck, and that, when under the influence of wine, it was his custom to sing directly into his hat, which he held out before him like a card tray. We will now begin." He whirled round, struck a few lugubrious notes and began to sing.

It was, as even Lane Parrington had to admit, extremely funny. He heard himself joining in the wild, deep roar of laughter that greeted the end of the first verse—he was annoyed at himself but he could not help it. By some magic, by some trick of gesture and voice, the chubby, bald-headed figure had suddenly become a large and lugubrious young man—a young man slightly under the influence of wine but still with the very best intentions, singing sentimentally and lugubriously into his hat. It was a trick and an act and a sleight of hand not worth learning—but it did not fail in its effect. Lane Parrington found himself laughing till he ached—beside him, the man named either Ferguson or Whitclaw was whooping and gasping for breath.

"And now," said Schooner Fairchild, while they were still laughing, "let somebody play who *can* play!" And, magically crooking his finger, he summoned a dark-haired undergraduate from the crowd, pushed him down on the piano stool, and, somehow or other, slipped through the press and vanished, while they were still calling his name.

Lane Parrington, a little later, found himself strolling up and down the dejected back yard of class headquarters. They had put up a tent, some iron tables and a number of paper lanterns, but, at this hour, the effect was not particularly gay. It must be very late and he ought to go to bed. But he did not look at his watch. He was trying to think about certain things in his life and get them into a proportion. It should be a simple thing to do, as simple as making money, but it was not.

Ted—Dorothy—the Leaf—Emmetsburg—Schooner Fairch-ild—Tom Drury—the place in Virginia and the mean house at Emmetsburg—United Investments and a sleight-of-hand trick at a tiny piano. He shuffled the factors of the equation about; they should add up to a whole. And, if they did, he would be willing to admit it; he told himself that. Yes, even if the final sum proved him wrong for years that had always been one of the factors of his own success, his knowing just when to cut a loss.

A shaky voice hummed behind him:

"Oh, the ship's cat said to the cabin boy,
To the cabin boy said she..."

He turned—it was Schooner Fairchild and, he thought at first, Schooner Fairchild was very drunk. Then he saw the man's lips were gray, caught him and helped him into one of the iron chairs.

"Sorry," wheezed Schooner Fairchild. "Must have run too fast, getting away from the gang. Damn' silly—left my medicine at the inn."

"Here—wait—" said Lane Parrington, remembering the flask of brandy in his pocket. He uncorked it and held it to the other man's lips. "Can you swallow?" he said solicitously.

An elfish, undefeated smile lit Schooner Fairchild's face. "Always could, from a child," he gasped. "Never ask a Fairchild twice." He drank and said, incredibly, it seemed to Lane Parrington, "Napoleon ... isn't it? Sir, you spoil me." His color began to come back. "Better," he said.

"Just stay there," said Lane Parrington. He dashed back into club headquarters—deserted now, he noticed, except for the gloomy caretaker and the man called Ferguson or Whitelaw, who was ungracefully asleep on a leather couch. Efficiently, he found glasses, ice, soda, plain water and ginger ale, and returned, his hands full of these trophies, to find Schooner Fairchild sitting up in his chair and attempting to get a cigarette from the pocket of his coat.

His eyes twinkled as he saw Lane Parrington's collection of glassware. "My!" he said, "We *are* going to make a night of it. Great shock to me—never thought it of you, Lane."

"Hadn't I better get a doctor?" said Lane Parrington. "There's a telephone—"

"Not a chance," said Schooner Fairchild. "It would worry Minnie sick. She made me promise before I came up to take care. It's just the old pump—misses a little sometimes. But I'll be all right, now—right as a trivet, whatever a trivet is. Just give me another shot of Napoleon."

"Of course," said Lane Parrington, "but—"

"Brandy on beer, never fear," said Schooner Fairchild. "Fairchild's Medical Maxims, Number One. And a cigarette ... thanks." He breathed deeply. "And there we are," he said, with a smile. "Just catches you in the short ribs, now and then. But, when it's over, it's over. You ought to try a little yourself, Lane—damn' silly performance of mine and you look tired."

"Thanks," said Lane Parrington, "I will." He made himself, neatly, an efficient brandy and soda and raised the glass to his lips. "Well—er—here's luck," he said, a little stiffly.

"Luck!" nodded Schooner Fairchild. They both drank. Lane Parrington looked at the pleasant, undefeated face.

"Listen, Schooner," said Lane Parrington, suddenly and harshly, "if you had the whole works to shoot over again—" He stopped.

"That's the hell of a question to ask a man at three o'clock in the morning," said Schooner equably. "Why?"

"Oh, I don't know," said Lane Parrington. "But that stuff at the piano you did—well, how did you do it?" His voice was oddly ingenious, for Lane Parrington.

"Genius, my boy, sheer, untrammeled genius," said Schooner Fairchild. He chuckled and sobered. "Well, somebody has to," he said reasonably. "And you wouldn't expect Tom Drury to do it, would you?—poor old Tom!"

"No," said Lane Parrington, breathing. "I wouldn't expect Tom Drury to do it."

"Oh, Tom's all right," said Schooner Fairchild. "He was just born with an ingrowing Drury and never had it operated on. But he's a fine guy, all the same. Lord," he said, "it must be a curse—to have to be a Drury, whether you like it or not. I never could have stood it—I never could have played the game. Of course," he added hastily, "I suppose it's different, if you do it all yourself, the way you have. That must be a lot of run."

"I wouldn't exactly call it fun," said Lane Parrington earnestly. "You see, after all, Schooner, there are quite a good many things that enter into…" He paused, and laughed hopelessly. "Was I always a stuffed shirt?" he said. "I suppose I was."

"Oh, I wouldn't call you a stuffed shirt," said Schooner, a little quickly. "You just had to succeed—and you've done it. Gosh, we all knew you were going to, right from the first— there couldn't be any mistake about that. It must be a swell feeling." He looked at Lane Parrington and his voice trailed off. He began again. "You see, it was different with me," he said. "I couldn't help it. Why, just take a look at me—I've even got a comedy face. Well, I never wanted anything very much except—oh, to have a good time and know other people were having a good time. Oh, I tried taking the other things seriously—I tried when I was a broker, but I couldn't, it was just no go. I made money enough—everybody was making money—but every now and then, in the middle of a million-share day, I'd just think how damn silly it was for everybody to be watching the board and getting all excited over things called

ATT and UGI. And that's no way for a broker to act—you've got to believe those silly initials mean something, if you want to be a broker.

"Well, I've tried a good many things since. And now and then I've been lucky, and we've gotten along. And I've spent most of Minnie's money, but she says it was worth it—and we've got the five girls and they're wonders—and I'll probably die playing the piano at some fool party, for you can't keep it up forever, but I only hope it happens before somebody says, 'There goes poor old Schooner. He used to be pretty amusing, in his time!' But, you see, I couldn't help it," he ended diffidently. "And, you know, I've tried. I've tried hard. But then I'd start laughing, and it always got in the way."

Lane Parrington looked at the man who had spent his wife's money and his own for a sleight-of-hand trick, five daughters, and the sound of friendly laughter. He looked at him without understanding, and yet with a curious longing.

"But, Schooner—" he said, "with all you can do—you ought to—"

"Oh," said Schooner, a trifle wearily, "one has one's dreams. Sure, I'd like to be Victor Boucher—he's a beautiful comedian. Or Bill Fields, for instance. Who wouldn't? But I don't kid myself. It's a parlor talent—it doesn't go over the footlights. But, Lord, what fun I've had with it! And the funny things people keep doing, forever and ever, amen. And the decent—the very decent things they keep doing, too. Well, I always thought it would be a good life, while you had it." He paused, and Lane Parrington saw the fatigue on his face. "Well, it's been a good party," he said. "I wish old Pozzy could have been here. But I guess we ought to go to bed."

"I'll phone for a cab," said Lane Parrington. "Nope—you're riding.

Lane Parrington shut the door of Schooner Fairchild's room behind him and stood, for a moment, with his hand on the knob. He had seen Schooner safely to bed—he had even insisted on the latter's taking his medicine, though Schooner had been a little petulant about it. Now, however, he still wondered about calling a doctor—if Schooner should be worse in the morning, he would have Anstey come up by plane. It was nothing to do, though not everybody could do it, and Anstey was much the best man. In any case, he would insist on Schooner's seeing Anstey this week. Then he wondered just how he was going to insist.

The old elevator just across the corridor came to a wheezing stop. Its door opened and a dark-haired girl in evening dress came out. Lane Parrington dropped his hand from the door-knob and turned away. But the girl took three quick steps after him.

"I'm sorry," she said, a little breathlessly, "but I'm Sylvia Fairchild. Is Father ill? The elevator boy said something—and I saw you coming out of his room,"

"He's all right," said Lane Parrington. "It was just the slightest sort of—"

"Oh!" said the girl, "do you mind coming back for a minute? You're Ted's father, aren't you? My room's next door, but I've got a key for his, too—Mother told me to be sure—" She seemed very self-possessed. Lane Parrington waited uncomfortably in the corridor for what seemed to him a long time, while she went into her father's room. When she came out again, she seemed relieved.

"It's all right," she said, in a low voice. "He's asleep, and his color's good. And he's…" She paused. "Oh, damn!" she said. "We can't talk out here. Come into my room for a minute—we can leave the door open—after all, you *are* Ted's father. I'll have to tell Mother, you see—and Father will just say it wasn't anything."

She opened the door and led the way into the room. "Here," she said. "Just throw those stockings off the chair—I'll sit on the bed. Well?"

"Well, I asked him if he wanted a doctor..." said Lane Parrington humbly.

When he had finished a concise, efficient report, the girl nodded, and he saw for the first time that she was pretty, with her dark, neat head and her clever, stubborn chin.

"Thank you," she said. "I mean, really. Father's a perfect lamb—but he doesn't like to worry Mother, and it worries her a lot more not to know. And sometimes it's rather difficult, getting the truth out of Father's friends. Not you," she was pleased to add. "You've been perfectly truthful. And the brandy was quite all right."

"I'm glad," said Lane Parrington. "I wish your father would see Anstey," he added, a trifle awkwardly. "I could—er—make arrangements."

"He has," said the girl. Her mouth twitched. "Oh," she said. "I shouldn't have gone to the dance. I couldn't help the Momus Club, but he might have come back afterward, if I'd been here. Only, I don't know."

"I wouldn't reproach myself," said Lane Parrington. "After all—"

"Oh, I know," said the girl. "After all! If you don't all manage to kill him, between you! Friends!" she sniffed. Then, suddenly, her face broke into lines of amusement. "I sound just like Aunt Emma," she said. "And that's pretty silly of me. Aunt Emma's almost pure poison. Of course it isn't your fault and I really do thank you. Very much. Do you know, I never expected you'd be a friend of Father's."

"After all," said Lane Parrington stiffly, "we were in the same class."

"Oh, I know," said the girl. "Father's talked about you, of course." Her mouth twitched again, but this time, it seemed to Lane Parrington, with a secret merriment. "And so has Ted, naturally," she added politely.

"I'm glad he happened to mention me," said Lane Parrington, and she grinned, frankly.

"I deserved that," she said, while Lane Parrington averted his eyes from what seemed to be a remarkably flimsy garment hung over the bottom of the bed. "But Ted has, really. He admires you quite a lot, you know, though, of course, you're different generations."

"Tell me—" said Lane Parrington. "No, I won't ask you."

"Oh, you know Ted," said the girl, rather impatiently. "It's awfully hard to get him to say things—and he will spend such a lot of time thinking he ought to be noble, poor lamb. But he's losing just a little of that, thank goodness—when he first came to Widgeon Point, he was trying so hard to be exactly like that terrible Drury boy. You see—" she said, suddenly and gravely, "he could lose quite a lot of it and still have more than most people."

Lane Parrington cleared his throat. There seemed nothing for him to say. Then he thought of something.

"His mother was—er—a remarkable person," he said. "We were not at all happy together. But she had remarkable qualities."

"Yes," said the girl. "Ted's told me. He remembers her." They looked at each other for a moment—he noted the stubborn chin, the swift and admirable hands. Then a clock on the mantel struck and the girl jumped.

"Good heavens!" she said. "It's four o'clock! Well—good night. And I do thank you, Mr. Parrington."

"It wasn't anything," said Lane Parrington. "But remember me to your father. But I'll see you in the morning, of course."

The following afternoon, Lane Parrington found himself waiting for his car in the lobby of the inn. There had been a little trouble with the garage and it was late. But he did not care, particularly, though he felt glad to be going back to New York. He had said good-by to Ted an hour before—Ted was going on to a house party at the Chiltons'—they'd eventually meet on Long Island, he supposed. Meanwhile, he had had a pleasant morning, attended the commencement exercises, and had lunch with Ted and the Fairchilds at the inn. Schooner had been a little subdued and both Ted and the girl frankly sleepy, but he had enjoyed the occasion nevertheless. And somehow the fact that the president's baccalaureate address had also viewed with alarm and talked about imperiled bulwarks and the American way of life—had, in fact, repeated with solemn precision a good many of the points in his own speech—did not irk Lane Parrington as it might nave the day before. After all, the boys were young and could stand it. They had stood a good deal of nonsense, even in his own time.

Now he thought once more of the equation he had tried too earnestly to solve, in the back yard of commencement headquarters—and, for a moment, almost grinned. It was, of course, insoluble—life was not as neat as that. You did what you could, as it was given you to do—very often you did the wrong things. And if you did the wrong things, you could hardly remedy them by a sudden repentance—or, at least, he could not. There were still the wigglers and the ones who stood still and each had his own virtues. And because he was a wiggler, he had thoughtfully and zealously done his best to make his son into the image of one of the magnificent sheep—the image of Tom Drury, who was neither hungry nor gay. He could not remedy that, but he thought he knew somebody who could remedy it, remembering the Fairchild girl's stubborn chin. And, in that case at least, the grandchildren ought to be worth watching.

"Your car, Mr. Parrington," said a bellboy. He moved toward the door. It was hard to keep from being a stuffed shirt, if you had the instinct in you, but one could try. A good deal might be done, with trying.

As he stepped out upon the steps of the inn, he noticed a figure, saluting—old Negro Mose, the campus character who remembered everybody's name.

"Hello, Mose!" said Lane Parrington. "Remember me?"

"Remember you—sho', Mr. Parrington," said Mose. He regarded Lane Parrington with beady eyes. "Let's see you was 1906."

"Nineteen hundred and eight," said Lane Parrington, but without rancor.

Mose gave a professional chuckle. "Sho'!" he said. "I was forgettin'! Let's see—you hasn't been back fo' years, Mister Parrington—but you was in Tom Drury's class an' Schooner Fairchild's class—"

"No," said Lane Parrington and gave the expected dollar, "not Tom Drury's class. Schooner Fairchild's class."

Everybody Was Very Nice
(1936)

Yes, I guess I have put on weight since you last saw me—not that you're any piker yourself, Spike. But I suppose you medicos have to keep in shape—probably do better than we downtown. I try to play golf in the week-ends, and I do a bit of sailing. But four innings of the baseball game at reunion was enough for me. I dropped out, after that, and let Art Corliss pitch.

You really should have been up there. After all, the Twentieth is quite a milestone—and the class is pretty proud of its famous man. What was it that magazine article said: "most brilliant young psychiatrist in the country"? I may not know psychiatry from marbles, but I showed it to Lisa, remarking that it was old Spike Garrett, and for once she was impressed. She thinks brokers are pretty dumb eggs. I wish you could stay for dinner—I'd like to show you the apartment and the twins. No, they're Lisa's and mine. Boys, if you'll believe it. Yes, the others are with Sally—young Barbara's pretty grown up, now.

Well, I can't complain. I may not be famous like you, Spike, but I manage to get along, in spite of the brain trusters, and having to keep up the place on Long Island. I wish you got East oftener—there's a pretty view from the guest house, right across the Sound—and if you wanted to write a book or anything, we'd know enough to leave you alone. Well, they started calling me a partner two years ago, so I guess that's what I am. Still fooling them, you know. But, seriously, we've got a pretty fine organization. We run a conservative business, but we're not all stuffed shirts, in spite of what the radicals say. As a matter of fact, you ought to see what the boys ran about us in the last Bawl Street Journal. Remind me to show it to you.

But it's your work I want to hear about—remember those bull-sessions we used to have in Old Main? Old Spike Garrett the Medical Marvel! Why, I've even read a couple of your books you old horse thief, believe it or not! You got me pretty tangled up on all that business about the id and the ego, too. But what I say is, there must be something in it if a fellow like Spike Garrett believes it. And there is, isn't there? Oh, I know you couldn't give me an answer in five minutes. But as long as there's a system—and the medicos know what they're doing.

I'm not asking for myself, of course—remember how you used to call me the 99 per-cent normal man? Well, I guess I haven't changed. It's just that I've gotten to thinking recently, and Lisa says I go around like a bear with a sore head. Well, it isn't that. I'm just thinking. A man has to think once in a while. And then, going back to reunion brought it all up again.

What I mean is this—the thing seemed pretty clear when we were in college. Of course, that was back in '15, but I can remember the way most of us thought. You fell in love with a girl and married her and settled down and had children and that was that. I'm not being simple-minded about it—you knew people get divorced, just as you knew people died, but it didn't seem something that was likely to happen to you. Especially if you came from a small Western city, as I did. Great Scott, I can remember when I was just a kid and the Prentisses got divorced. They were pretty prominent people and it shook the whole town.

That's why I want to figure things out for my own satisfaction. Because I never expected to be any Lothario—I'm not the type. And yet Sally and I got divorced and we're both remarried, and even so, to tell you the truth, things aren't going too well. I'm not saying a word against Lisa. But that's the way things are. And it isn't as if I were the only one. You can look around anywhere and see it, and it starts you wondering.

I'm not going to bore you about myself and Sally. Good Lord, you ushered at the wedding, and she always liked you. Remember when you used to come out to the house? Well, she hasn't changed—she's still got that little smile—though, of course, we're all older. Her husband's a doctor, too—that's funny, isn't it?—and they live out in Montclair. They've got a nice place there and he's very well thought of. We used to live in Meadowfield, remember?

I remember the first time I saw her after she married McConaghey—oh, we're perfectly friendly, you know. She had on red nail polish and her hair was different, a different bob. And she had one of those handbags with her new initials on it. It's funny, the first time, seeing your wife in clothes you don't know. Though Lisa and I have been married eight years, for that matter, and Sally and I were divorced in '28.

Of course, we have the children for part of the summer. We'll have Barbara this summer—Bud'll be in camp. It's a little difficult sometimes, but we all co-operate. You have to. And there's plenty to do on Long Island in the summer, that's one thing. But they and Lisa get along very well—Sally's brought them up nicely that way. For that matter, Doctor McConaghey's very nice when I see him. He gave me a darn good prescription for a cold and I get it filled every winter. And Jim Blake—he's Lisa's first husband—is really pretty interesting, now we've got to seeing him again. In fact, we're all awfully nice—just as nice and polite as we can be. And sometimes I get to wondering if it mightn't be a good idea if somebody started throwing fits and shooting rockets, instead. Of course I don't really mean that.

You were out for a week end with us in Meadowfield—maybe you don't remember it—but Bud was about six months old then and Barbara was just running around. It wasn't a bad house, if you remember the house. Dutch Colonial, and the faucet in the pantry leaked. The landlord was always fixing it, but he never quite fixed it right. And you had to cut hard to the left to back into the garage. But Sally liked the Japanese cherry tree and it wasn't a bad house. We were going to build on Rose Hill Road eventually. We had the lot picked out, if we didn't have the money, and we made plans about it. Sally never could remember to put in the doors in the plan, and we laughed about that.

It wasn't anything extraordinary, just an evening. After supper, we sat around the lawn in deck chairs and drank Sally's beer—it was long before Repeal. We'd repainted the deck chairs ourselves the Sunday before and we felt pretty proud of them. The light stayed late, but there was a breeze after dark, and once Bud started yipping and Sally went up to him. She had on a white dress, I think—she used to wear white a lot in the summers—it went with her blue eyes and her yellow hair. Well, it wasn't anything extraordinary—we didn't even stay up late. But we were all there. And if you'd told me that within three years we'd both be married to other people, I'd have thought you were raving.

Then you went West, remember, and we saw you off on the train. So you didn't see what happened, and, as a matter of fact, it's hard to remember when we first started meeting the Blakes. They'd moved to Meadowfield then, but we hadn't met them.

Jim Blake was one of those pleasant, ugly-faced people with steel glasses who get right ahead in the law and never look young or old. And Lisa was Lisa. She's dark, you know, and she takes a beautiful burn. She was the first girl there to wear real beach things or drink a special kind of tomato juice when everybody else was drinking cocktails. She was very pretty and very good fun to be with—she's got lots of ideas. They entertained a good deal because Lisa likes that—she had her own income, of course, and she and Jim used to bicker a good deal in public in an amusing way—it was sort of an act or seemed like it. They had one little girl, Sylvia, that Jim was crazy about. I mean it sounds normal, doesn't it, even to their having the kind of Airedale you had then? Well, it all seemed normal enough to us, and they soon got to be part of the crowd. You know, the young married crowd in every suburb.

Of course, that was '28 and the boom was booming and everybody was feeling pretty high. I suppose that was part of it—the money—and the feeling you had that everything was going faster and faster and wouldn't stop. Why, it was Sally herself who said that we owed ourselves a whirl and mustn't get stodgy and settled while we were still young. Well, we had snick pretty close to the grindstone for the past few years, with the children and everything. And it was fun to feel young and sprightly again and buy a new car and take in the club gala without having to worry about how you'd pay your house account. But I don't see any harm in that.

And then, of course, we talked and kidded a lot about freedom and what have you. Oh, you know the kind of talk—everybody was talking it then. About not being Victorians and living your own life. And there was the older generation and the younger generation. I've forgotten a lot of it now, but I remember there was one piece about love not being just a form of words mumbled by a minister, but something pretty special. As a matter of fact, the minister who married us was old Doctor Snell and he had the kind of voice you could hear in the next county. But I used to talk about that mumbling minister myself. I mean, we were enlightened, for a suburb, if you get my point. Yes, and pretty proud of it, too. When they banned a book in Boston, the lending library ordered six extra copies. And I still remember the big discussion we had about perfect freedom in marriage when even the straight Republicans voted the radical ticket. All except Chick Bewleigh, and he was a queer sort of bird, who didn't even believe that stocks had reached a permanently high plateau.

But, meanwhile, most of us were getting the 8:15 and our wives were going down to the chain store and asking if that was a really nice head of lettuce. At least that's the way we seemed. And, if the crowd started kidding me about Mary Sennett, or Mac Church kissed Sally on the ear at a club revel, why, we were young, we were modern, and we could handle that. I wasn't going to take a shotgun to Mac, and Sally wasn't going to put on the jealous act. Oh, we had it all down to a science. We certainly did.

Good Lord, we had the Blakes to dinner, and they had us. They'd drop over for drinks or we'd drop over there. It was all perfectly normal and part of the crowd. For that matter, Sally played with Jim Blake in the mixed handicap and they got to the semifinals. No, I didn't play with Lisa—she doesn't like golf. I mean that's the way it was.

And I can remember the minute it started, and it wasn't anything, just a party at the Bewleighs'. They've got a big, rambling house and people drift around. Lisa and I had wandered out to the kitchen to get some drinks for the people on the porch. She had on a black dress, that night, with a big sort of orange flower on it. It wouldn't have suited everybody, but it suited her.

We were talking along like anybody and suddenly we stopped talking and looked at each other. And I felt, for a minute, well, just the way I felt when I was first in love with Sally. Only this time, it wasn't Sally. It happened so suddenly that all I could think of was, "Watch your step!" Just as if you'd gone into a room in the dark and hit your elbow. I guess that makes it genuine, doesn't it?

We picked it up right away and went back to the party. All she said was, "Did anybody ever tell you that you're really quite a menace, Dan?" and she said that in the way we all said those things. But, all the same, it had happened. I could hear her voice all the way back in the car. And yet, I was as fond of Sally as ever. I don't suppose you'll believe that, but it's true.

And next morning, I tried to kid myself that it didn't have any importance. Because Sally wasn't jealous, and we were all modern and advanced and knew about life. But the next time I saw Lisa, I knew it had.

I want to say this. If you think it was all romance and rosebuds, you're wrong. A lot of it was merry hell. And yet, everybody whooped us on. That's what I don't understand. They didn't really want the Painters and the Blakes to get divorced, and yet they were pretty interested. Now, why do people do that? Some of them would carefully put Lisa and me next to each other at table and some of them would just as carefully not. But it all added up to the same thing in the end—a circus was going on and we were part of the circus. It's interesting to watch the people on the high wires at the circus and you hope they don't fall. But, if they did, that would be interesting too. Of course, there were a couple of people who tried, as they say, to warn us. But they were older people and just made us mad.

Everybody was so nice and considerate and understanding. Everybody was so nice and intelligent and fine. Don't misunderstand me. It was wonderful, being with Lisa. It was new and exciting. And it seemed to be wonderful for her, and she'd been unhappy with Jim. So, anyway, that made me feel less of a heel, though I felt enough of a heel, from time to time. And then, when we were together, it would seem so fine.

A couple of times we really tried to break it, too—at least twice. But we all belonged to the same crowd, and what could you do but run away? And, somehow, that meant more than running away—it meant giving in to the Victorians and that mumbling preacher and all the things we'd said we didn't believe in. Or I suppose Sally might have done like old Mrs. Pierce, back home. She horsewhipped the dressmaker on the station platform and then threw herself crying into Major Pierce's arms and he took her to Atlantic City instead. It's one of the town's great stories and I always wondered what they talked about on the train. Of course, they moved to Des Moines after that—I remember reading about their golden wedding anniversary when I was in college. Only nobody could do that nowadays, and, besides, Lisa wasn't a dressmaker.

So, finally, one day, I came home, and there was Sally, perfectly cold, and, we talked pretty nearly all night. We'd been awfully polite to each other for quite a while before—the way you are. And we kept polite, we kept a good grip on ourselves. After all, we'd said to each other before we were married that if either of us ever—and there it was. And it was Sally who brought that up, not me. I think we'd have felt better if we'd fought. But we didn't fight.

Of course, she was bound to say some things about Lisa, and I was bound to answer. But that didn't last long and we got our grip right back again. It was funny, being strangers and talking so politely, but we did it. I think it gave us a queer .kind of pride to do it. I think it gave us a queer kind of pride for her to ask me politely for a drink at the end, as if she were in somebody else's house, and for me to mix it for her, as if she were a guest.

Everything was talked out by then and the house felt very dry and empty, as if nobody lived in it at all. We'd never been up quite so late in the house, except after a New Year's party or when Buddy was sick, that time. I mixed her drink very carefully, the way she liked it, with plain water, and she took it and said "Thanks." Then she sat for a while without saying anything. It was so quiet you could hear the little drip of the leaky faucet in the pantry, in spite of the door being closed. She heard it and said, "It's dripping again. You better call up Mr. Vye in the morning—I forgot. And I think Barbara's getting a cold—I meant to tell you." Then her face twisted and I thought she was going to cry, but she didn't.

She put the glass down—she'd only drunk half her drink— and said, quite quietly, "Oh, damn you, and damn Lisa Blake, and damn everything in the world!" Then she ran upstairs before I could stop her and she still wasn't crying.

I could have run upstairs after her, but I didn't. I stood looking at the glass on the table and I couldn't think. Then, after a while, I heard a key turn in a lock. So I picked up my hat and went out for a walk—I hadn't been out walking that early in a long time. Finally, I found an all-night diner and got some coffee. Then I came back and read a book that the maid got down—it wasn't a very interesting book. When she came down, I pretended I'd gotten up early and had to go into town by the first train, but I guess she knew.

I'm not going to talk about the details. If you've been through them, you've been through them; and if you haven't, you don't know. My family was fond of Sally, and Sally's had always liked me. Well, that made it tough. And the children. They don't say the things you expect them to. I'm not going to talk about that.

Oh, we put on a good act, we put on a great show! There weren't any fists flying or accusations. Everybody said how well we did it, everybody in town. And Lisa and Sally saw each other, and Jim Blake and I talked to each other perfectly calmly. We said all the usual things. He talked just as if it were a case. I admired him for it. Lisa did her best to make it emotional, but we wouldn't let her. And I finally made her see that, court or no court, he'd simply have to have Sylvia. He was crazy about her, and while Lisa's a very good mother, there wasn't any question as to which of them the kid liked best. It happens that way, sometimes.

For that matter, I saw Sally off on the train to Reno. She wanted it that way. Lisa was going to get a Mexican divorce—they'd just come in, you know. And nobody could have told, from the way we talked in the station. It's funny, you get a queer bond, through a time like that. After I'd seen her off—and she looked small in the train—the first person I wanted to see wasn't Lisa, but Jim Blake. You see, other people are fine, but unless you've been through things yourself, you don't quite understand them. But Jim Blake was still in Meadowfield, so I went back to the club.

I hadn't ever really lived in the club before, except for three days one summer. They treat you very well, but, of course, being a college club, it's more for the youngsters and the few old boys who hang around the bar. I got awfully tired of the summer chintz in the dining room and the Greek waiter I had who breathed on my neck. And you can't work all the time, though I used to stay late at the office. I guess it was then I first thought of getting out of Spencer Wilde and making a new connection. You think about a lot of things at a time like that.

Of course, there were lots of people I could have seen, but I didn't much want to—somehow, you don't. Though I did strike up quite a friendship with one of the old boys. He was about fifty-five and he'd been divorced four times and was living permanently at the club. We used to sit up in his little room—he'd had his own furniture moved in and the walls were covered with pictures—drinking Tom Collinses and talking about life. He had lots of ideas about life, and about matrimony, too, and I got quite interested, listening to him. But then he'd go into the dinners he used to give at Delmonico's, and while that was interesting, too, it wasn't much help, except to take your mind off the summer chintz.

He had sonic sort of small job, downtown, but I guess he had an income from his family too. He must have. But when I'd ask him what he did, he'd always say, "I'm retired, my boy, very much retired, and how about a touch more beverage to keep out the sun?" He always called it beverage, but they knew what he meant at the bar. He turned up at the wedding, when Lisa and I were married, all dressed up in a cutaway, and insisted on making us a little speech—very nice it was too. Then we had him to dinner a couple of times, after we'd got back, and somehow or other, I haven't seen him since. I suppose he's still at the club—I've got out of the habit of going there, since I joined the other ones, though I still keep my membership.

Of course, all that time, I was crazy about Lisa and writing her letters and waiting till we could be married. Of course I was. But, now and then, even that would get shoved into the background. Because there was so much to do and arrangements to make and people like lawyers to see. I don't like lawyers very much, even yet, though the people we had were very good. But there was all the telephoning and the conferences. Somehow, it was like a machine—a big machine—and you had to learn a sort of new etiquette for everything you did. Till, finally, it got so that about all you wanted was to have the fuss over and not talk about it any more.

I remember running into Chick Bewleigh in the club, three days before Sally got her decree. You'd like Chick—he's the intellectual type, but a darn good fellow too. And Nan, his wife, is a peach—one of those big, rangy girls with a crazy sense of humor. It was nice to talk to him because he was natural and didn't make any cracks about grass-bachelors or get that look in his eye. You know the look they get. We talked about Meadowfield—just the usual news—the Bakers were splitting up and Don Sikes had a new job and the Wilsons were having a baby. But it seemed good to hear it.

"For that matter," he said, drawing on his pipe, "we're adding to the population again ourselves. In the fall. How we'll ever manage four of them! I keep telling Nan she's cockeyed, but she says they're more fun than a swimming pool and cost less to keep up, so what can you do!"

He shook his head and I remembered that Sally always used to say she wanted six. Only now it would be Lisa, so I mustn't think about that.

"So that's your recipe for a happy marriage," I said. "Well, I always wondered."

I was kidding, of course, but he looked quite serious.

"*Kinder, Küche und Kirche?*" he said. "Nope, that doesn't work any more, what with pre-schools, automats and the movies. Four children or no four children, Nan could still raise hell if she felt like raising hell. And so could I, for that matter. Add blessings of civilization," and his eyes twinkled.

"Well then," I said, "what is it?" I really wanted to know.

"Oh, just bull luck, I suppose. And happening to like what you've got," he answered, in a sort of embarrassed way.

"You can do that," I said. "And yet—"

He looked away from me.

"Oh, it was a lot simpler in the old days," he said. "Everything was for marriage—church, laws, society. And when people got married, they expected to stay that way. And it made a lot of people as unhappy as hell. Now the expectation's rather the other way, at least in this great and beautiful nation and among people like us. If you get a divorce, it's rather like going to the dentist—unpleasant sometimes, but lots of people have been there before. Well, that's a handsome system, too, but it's got its own casualty list. So there you are. You takes your money and you makes your choice. And some of us like freedom better than the institution and some of us like the institution better, but what most of us would like is to be Don Juan on Thursdays and Benedick, the married man, on Fridays, Saturdays and the rest of the week. Only that's a bit hard to work out, somehow," and he grinned.

"All the same," I said, "you and Nan—"

"Well," he said, "I suppose we're exceptions. You see, my parents weren't married till I was seven. So I'm a conservative. It might have worked out the other way."

"Oh," I said.

"Yes," he said. "My mother was English, and you may have heard of English divorce laws. She ran away with my father and she was perfectly right—her husband was a very extensive brute. All the same, I was brought up on the other side of the fence, and I know something about what it's like. And Nan was a minister's daughter who thought she ought to be free. Well, we argued about things a good deal. And, finally, I told her that I'd be very highly complimented to live with her on any terms at all, but if she wanted to get married, she'd have to expect a marriage, not a trip to Coney Island. And I made my point rather clear by blacking her eye, in a taxi, when she told me she was thinking seriously of spending a week end with my deadly rival, just to see which one of us she really loved. You can't spend a romantic week end with somebody when you've got a black eye. But you can get married with one and we did. She had raw beefsteak on it till two hours before the wedding, and it was the prettiest sight I ever saw. Well, that's our simple story."

"Not all of it," I said.

"No," he said, "not all of it. But at least we didn't start in with any of this bunk about if you meet a handsomer fellow it's all off. We knew we were getting into something. Bewleigh's Easy Guide to Marriage in three installments—you are now listening to the Voice of Experience, and who cares? Of course, if we hadn't—ahem—liked each other, I could have blacked her eye till doomsday and got nothing out of it but a suit for assault and battery. But nothing's much good unless it's worth fighting for. And she doesn't look exactly like a downtrodden wife."

"Nope," I said, "but all the same—"

He stared at me very hard almost the way he used to when people were explaining that stocks had reached a permanently high plateau.

"Exactly," he said. "And there comes a time, no matter what the intention, when a new face heaves into view and a spark lights. I'm no Adonis, God knows, but it's happened to me once or twice. And I know what I do then. I run. I run like a rabbit. It isn't courageous or adventurous or fine. It isn't even particularly moral, as I think about morals. But I run. Because, when all's said and done, it takes two people to make a love affair and you can't have it when one of them's not there. And, dammit, Nan knows it, that's the trouble. She'd ask Helen of Troy to dinner just to see me run. Well, good-by, old man, and our best to Lisa, of course—"

After he was gone, I went and had dinner in the grill. I did a lot of thinking at dinner, but it didn't get me anywhere. When I was back in the room, I took the receiver off the telephone. I was going to call long distance. But your voice sounds different on the phone, and, anyway, the decree would be granted in three days. So when the girl answered, I told her it was a mistake.

Next week Lisa came back and she and I were married. We went to Bermuda on our wedding trip. It's a very pretty place. Do you know, they won't allow an automobile on the island?

The queer thing was that at first I didn't feel married to Lisa at all. I mean, on the boat, and even at the hotel. She said, "But how exciting, darling!" and I suppose it was.

Now, of course, we've been married eight years, and that's always different. The twins will be seven in May—two years older than Sally's Jerry. I had an idea for a while that Sally might marry Jim Blake—he always admired her. But I'm glad she didn't—it would have made things a little too complicated. And I like Mc-Conaghey—I like him fine. We gave them an old Chinese jar for a wedding present. Lisa picked it out. She has very good taste and Sally wrote us a fine letter.

I'd like to have you meet Lisa sometime—she's interested in intelligent people. They're always coming to the apartment—artists and writers and people like that.

Of course, they don't always turn out the way she expects. But she's quite a hostess and she knows how to handle things. There was one youngster that used to rather get in my hair. He'd call me the Man of Wall Street and ask me what I thought about Picabia or one of those birds, in a way that sort of said, "Now watch this guy stumble!" But as soon as Lisa noticed it, she got rid of him. That shows she's considerate.

Of course, it's different, being married to a person. And I'm pretty busy these days and so is she. Sometimes, if I get home and there's going to be a party, I'll just say good night to the twins and fade out after dinner. But Lisa understands about that, and I've got my own quarters. She had one of her decorator friends do the private study and it really looks very nice.

I had Jim Blake in there one night. Well) I had to take him somewhere. He was getting pretty noisy and Lisa gave me the high sign. He's doing very well, but he looks pretty hard these days and I'm afraid he's drinking a good deal, though he doesn't often show it. I don't think he ever quite got over Sylvia's dying. Four years ago. They had scarlet fever at the school. It was a great shock to Lisa, too, of course, but she had the twins and Jim never married again. But he comes to see us, every once in a while. Once, when he was tight, he said it was to convince himself about remaining a bachelor, but I don't think he meant that.

Now, when I brought him into the study, he looked around and said, "Shades of Buck Rogers! What one of Lisa's little dears produced this imitation Wellsian nightmare?"

"Oh, I don't remember," I said. "I think his name was Slivovitz."

"It looks as if it had been designed by a man named Slivovitz," he said. "All dental steel and black glass. I recognize the Lisa touch. You're lucky she didn't put murals of cogwheels on the walls."

"Well, there was a question of that," I said.

"I bet there was," he said. "Well, here's how, old man! Here's to two great big wonderful institutions, marriage and divorce!"

I didn't like that very much and told him so. But he just wagged his head at me.

"I like you, Painter," he said. "I always did. Sometimes I think you're goofy, but I like you. You can't insult me—I won't let you. And it isn't your fault."

"What isn't my fault?" I said.

"The setup," he said. "Because, in your simple little heart, you're an honest monogamous man, Painter—monogamous as most. And if you'd stayed married to Sally, you'd have led an honest monogamous life. But they loaded the dice against you, out at Meadowfield, and now Lord knows where you'll end up.

After all, I was married to Lisa myself for six years or so. Tell me, isn't it hell?"

"You're drunk," I said.

"*In vino veritas*" said he. "No, it isn't hell—I take that back. Lisa's got her damn-fool side, but she's an attractive and interesting woman—or could be, if she'd work at it. But she was brought up on the idea of Romance with a big R, and she's too bone-lazy and bone-selfish to work at it very long. There's always something else, just over the horizon. Well, I got tired of fighting that, after a while. And so will you. She doesn't want husbands—she wants clients and followers. Or maybe you're tired already."

"I think you'd better go home, Jim," I said. "I don't want to have to ask you."

"Sorry," he said. "*In vino veritas.* But it's a funny setup, isn't it? What Lisa wanted was a romantic escapade—and she got twins. And what you wanted was marriage—and you got Lisa. As for me," and for a minute his face didn't look drunk any more, "what I principally wanted was Sylvia and I've lost that. I could have married again, but I didn't think that'd be good for her. Now, I'll probably marry some client I've helped with her decree—we don't touch divorce, as a rule, just a very, very special line of business for a few important patrons. I know those—I've had them in the office. And won't that be fun for us all! What a setup it is!" and he slumped down in his chair and went to sleep. I let him sleep for a while and then had Briggs take him down in the other elevator. He called up next day and apologized—said he knew he must have been noisy, though he couldn't remember anything he said.

The other time I had somebody in the study was when Sally came back there once, two years ago. We'd met to talk about college for Barbara and I'd forgotten some papers I wanted to show her. We generally meet downtown. But she didn't mind coming back—Lisa was out, as it happened. It made me feel queer, taking her up in the elevator and letting her in at the door. She wasn't like Jim—she thought the study was nice.

Well, we talked over our business and I kept looking at her. You can see she's older, but her eyes are still that very bright blue, and she bites her thumb when she's interested. It's a queer feeling. Of course, I was used to seeing her, but we usually met downtown. You know, I wouldn't have been a bit surprised if she'd pushed the bell and said, "Tea, Briggs, I'm home." She didn't, naturally.

I asked her, once, if she wouldn't take off her hat and she looked at me in a queer way and said, "So you can show me your etchings? Dan, Dan, you're a dangerous man!" and for a moment we both laughed like fools.

"Oh, dear," she said, drying her eyes, "that's very funny. And now I must be going home."

"Look here, Sally," I said, "I've always told you—but, honestly, if you need anything—if there's anything—"

"Of course, Dan," she said. "And we're awfully good friends, aren't we?" But she was still smiling.

I didn't care. "Friends!" I said. "You know how I think about you. I always have. And I don't want you to think—"

She patted my shoulder—I'd forgotten the way she used to do that.

"There," she said. "Mother knows all about it. And we really are friends, Dan. So—"

"I was a fool."

She looked at me very steadily out of those eyes.

"We were all fools," she said. "Even Lisa. I used to hate her for a while. I used to hope things would happen to her. Oh, not very bad things. Just her finding out that you never see a crooked picture without straightening it, and hearing you say: 'A bird can't fly on one wing,' for the dozenth time. The little things everybody has to find out and put up with. But I don't even do that any more."

"If you'd ever learned to put a cork back in a bottle," I said. "I mean the right cork in the right bottle. But—"

"I do so! No, I suppose I never will." And she laughed. She took my hands. "Funny, funny, funny," she said. "And funny to have it all gone and be friends."

"Is it all gone? "I said.

"Why, no, of course not," she said. "I don't suppose it ever is, quite. Like the boys who took you to dances. And there's the children, and you can't help remembering. But it's gone. We had it and lost it. I should have fought for it more, I suppose, but I didn't. And then I was terribly hurt and terribly mad. But I got over that. And now I'm married to Jerry. And I wouldn't give him up, or Jerry Junior, for anything in the world. The only thing that worries me is sometimes when I think it isn't quite a fair deal for him. After all, he could have married—well, some-body else. And yet he knows I love him."

"He ought to," I said rather stiffly. "He's a darn lucky guy, if you ask me."

"No, Dan, I'm the lucky girl. I'm hoping this minute that Mrs. Potter's X-rays turn out all right. He did a beautiful job on her. But he always worries."

I dropped her hands.

"Well, give him my best," I said.

"I will, Dan. He likes you, you know. Really he does. By the way, have you had any more of that bursitis? There's a new treat-ment he wanted me to ask you—"

"Thanks," I said, "but that all cleared up." .

"I'm glad. And now I must fly. There's always shopping when

you come in from the suburbs. Give my best to Lisa and tell her was sorry not to see her. She's out, I suppose."

"Yes," I said. "She'll be sorry to miss you—you wouldn't stay for a cocktail? She's usually in around then."

"It sounds very dashing, but I mustn't. Jerry Junior lost one of his turtles and I've got to get him another. Do you know a good pet shop? Well, Bloomingdale's, I suppose—after all, I've got other things to get."

"There's a good one two blocks down on Lexington," I said. "But if you're going to Bloomingdale's—Well, good-by, Sally, and good luck."

"Good-by, Dan. And good luck to you. And no regrets."

"No regrets," I said, and we shook hands.

There wasn't any point in going down to the street with her, and besides I had to phone the office. But before I did, I looked out, and she was just getting into a cab. A person looks different, somehow, when they don't know you're seeing them. I could see the way she looked to other people—not young any more, not the Sally I'd married, not even the Sally I'd talked with, all night in that cold house. She was a nice married woman who lived in Montclair and whose husband was a doctor; a nice woman, in shopping for the day, with a new spring hat and a fifty-trip ticket in her handbag. She'd had trouble in her life, but she'd worked it out. And, before she got on the train, she'd have a black-and- white soda, sitting on a stool at the station, or maybe she didn't do that any more. There'd be lots of things in her handbag, but I wouldn't know about any of them nor what locks the keys fitted. And, if she were dying, they'd send for me, because that would be etiquette. And the same if I were dying. But we'd had something and lost it—the way she said—and that was all that was left.

Now she was that nice Mrs. McConaghey. But she'd never

be quite that to me. And yet, there was no way to go back. You couldn't even go back to the house in Meadowfield—they'd torn it down and put up an apartment instead.

So that's why I wanted to talk to you. I'm not complaining and I'm not the kind of fellow that gets nerves. But I just want to know—I just want to figure it out. And sometimes it keeps going round and round in your head. You'd like to be able to tell your children something, especially when they're growing up. Well, I know what we'll tell them. But I wonder if it's enough.

Not that we don't get along well when Bud and Barbara come to see us. Especially Barbara—she's very tactful and she's crazy about the twins. And now they're growing up, it's easier. Only, once in a while, something happens that makes you think. I took Barbara out sailing last summer. She's sixteen and a very sweet kid, if I say it myself. A lot of kids that age seem pretty hard, but she isn't.

Well, we were just talking along, and, naturally, you like to know what your children's plans are. Bud thinks he wants to be a doctor like McConaghey and I've no objection. I asked Barbara if she wanted a career, but she said she didn't think so.

"Oh, I'd like to go to college," she said, "and maybe work for a while, afterwards, the way mother did, you know. But I haven't any particular talents, dad. I could kid myself, but I haven't. I guess it's just woman's function and home and babies for me."

"Well, that sounds all right to me," I said, feeling very paternal.

"Yes," she said, "I like babies. In fact, I think I'll get married pretty young, just for the experience. The first time probably won't work, but it ought to teach you some things. And then, eventually, you might find somebody to tie to."

"So that's the way it is with the modern young woman?" I said.

"Why, of course," she said. "That's what practically all the girls say—we've talked it all over at school. Of course, sometimes it takes you quite a while. Like Helen Hastings' mother. She just got married for the fourth time last year, but he really is a sweet! He took us all to the matinee when I was visiting Helen and we nearly died. He's a count, of course, and he's got the darlingest accent. I don't know whether I'd like a count, though it must be fun to have little crowns on your handkerchiefs like Helen's mother. What's the matter, daddy? Are you shocked?"

"Don't flatter yourself, young lady—I've been shocked by experts," I said. "No, I was just thinking. Suppose we—well, suppose your mother and I had stayed together? How would you have felt about it then?"

"But you didn't, did you?" she said, and her voice wasn't hurt or anything, just natural. "I mean, almost nobody does any more. Don't worry, daddy. Bud and I understand all about it—good gracious, we're grown up! Of course, if you and mother had," she said, rather dutifully, "I suppose it would have been very nice. But then we'd have missed Mac, and he really is a sweet, and you'd have missed Lisa and the twins. Anyhow, it's all worked out now. Oh, of course, I'd rather hope it would turn out all right the first time, if it wasn't too stodgy or sinister. But you've got to face facts, you know."

"Face facts!" I said. "Dammit, Barbara!"

Then I stopped, because what did I have to say?

Well, that's the works, and if you've got any dope on it, I wish you'd tell me. There are so few people you can talk to—that's the trouble. I mean everybody's very nice, but that's not the same thing. And, if you start thinking too much, the highballs catch up on you. And you can't afford that—I've never been much of a drinking man.

The only thing is, where does it stop, if it does? That's the thing I'm really afraid of.

It may sound silly to you. But I've seen other people—well, take this Mrs. Hastings, Barbara talked about. Or my old friend at the club. I wonder if he started in, wanting to get married four times. I know I didn't—I'm not the type and you know it.

And yet, suppose, well, you do meet somebody who treats you like a human being. I mean somebody who doesn't think you're a little goofy because you know more about American Can than who painted what. Supposing, even, they're quite a lot younger. That shouldn't make all the difference. After all, I'm no Lothario. And Lisa and I aren't thinking of divorce or anything like that. But, naturally, we lead our own lives, and you ought to be able to talk to somebody. Of course, if it could have been Sally. That was my fault. But it isn't as if Maureen were just in the floor show. She's got her own specialty number. And, really, when you get to know her, she's a darned intelligent kid.

ALL AROUND THE TOWN

(1940)

I

I LIKE IT, winter or summer. But I guess I like it the best when it gets really hot and they turn on the fire hydrants for a while and the little kids splash in the water. That's when the noise lasts till after twelve and, if you look out of the window, you can see a man in his shirt sleeves and his fat wife beside him, sitting out in front of the store in a couple of kitchen chairs. I know nobody's supposed to. But that's the way I like New York.

No, I was born in Brooklyn, but I don't remember much about that. We moved to the East Side afterwards, before I could remember. The old man was a watch repairer—I guess that's where I get my liking for tinkering at things. He worked at Logan's, up on Fourteenth, and I remember how disappointed I was when I found he didn't own the whole store. He was Swiss and Ma was Irish, so I've got the two sides to me. They get along well enough, usually, but sometimes they fight.

I know now he had disappointments, but I didn't know it as a kid. He was always talking about a nice place in the country, with chickens, but he never got there. Once or twice, before I was born,—I came along kind of later,—he tried to set up in a small town. But something always happened, and he had to come back to the city. He didn't really object to it, but he felt it wasn't right to raise his kids there. But Ma always said it was up to her to take care of that. She did a good job by us, too, and she kissed me on both sides of my face when I got the silver medal for penmanship at St. Aloysius's. I didn't tell her it was because I'd promised Jerry Toole I'd beat the mush off him if he came in ahead of me. He was always the one to get the prizes, and I thought it was time I had one of my own to take home and show. My old man made a little wooden box for it and carved my initials on top. It took him quite a little while to do it,—he was a slow worker, but very careful,—but it pleased him a lot. And me, too.

I guess I don't know how to tell a story, because, when I think about it, it gets all mixed up. They ask you what was the city like, in those days, and what are you going to tell them? I remember the horsecars, to be sure, and the gaslights in the streets, and the tangle of overhead wires, like a crazy spiderweb, and the big white stages. But, when you begin thinking back, you don't know if you're right or not. My old man had big gray moustaches that went out like a pair of wings, and he always wore a derby hat to his work. It was rounder, somehow, than they make derbies now—I'd recognize it among a million, but they don't have them any more. And, when Ma was baking, you could smell the clean, fresh bread all over the house. The first policeman I ever saw was standing under a gaslight, twirling his stick in front of his belly. We called him Mister Ryan and I thought him the greatest and largest man in the world. Well, that's the thing you remember. That, and the sprinkling carts, and the brown afternoon in the street, and the old woman who sold hot chestnuts, with her cheeks as red as red apples, a winter evening, under the El, when the horses were slipping on the ice.

All the same, it wasn't so big, then. I remember when the Flatiron was the biggest one and the out-of-town people bought postcards, just the way they do, this moment, with the Empire State. It got built without our knowing it, almost—it went up into the sky. Nobody decided about it—it stretched like a boy growing up, and now, there it is. The city, I mean—yes, the city. I remember my tall, laughing Irish uncles stamping into the house and swinging Ma from one to another of them and kissing her till she'd slap their faces. She was always little Katy, the bird, to them, though she'd had a great hand in bringing most of them up. I remember when Uncle Ally got in the Fire Department and his coming around, proud as Punch, to show us his new uniform. A well-set-up man he was, and his helmet very impressive. He was killed in a big loft fire in the garment district, the year that I was sixteen. The whole wall fell like a stone and they couldn't get the bodies for two days.

All the same, they gave the three of them a Department funeral and there were pieces in all the papers about it. I think it helped break Ma's heart—he was her favorite brother. But I rode in the carriage with her and she sat up straight as a ramrod, in her new black clothes. Afterwards she had me cut the pieces out of the papers, and it wasn't till night that I heard her crying. I can hear the cry in my ears, though it's many years gone.

My old man and my uncles were polite enough to each other, but they didn't really get along. He liked to sit out on the stoop, after dinner, smoking his big pipe with the silver lid on it and reading the evening paper. But he was a quiet man, and when my uncles came in, full of life and gayety, he'd have less to say than ever, though he always sent to the corner for the beer. He'd never have a drop of whiskey in the house, except for medical purposes—but he liked the steam beer at Schaeffer's, though I never saw him take too much. The day he came home with the chill, Ma made him a toddy, but even then he wouldn't take it. It scared me to see him in bed in the daytime, with his red-bordered nightshirt on. When you're young, you never think your parents can get sick or die. I remember that. But he got over it; and it wasn't till after I was married that he died.

He liked Eileen and she was very good to him—I'll always remember that. She used to call him Father Weiss,—she was dainty in her conversation,—but he'd always say, "Joost Poppa, *mein liebliches Kind*" Then he'd stroke her hand, very gently, with the tips of his big, clever fingers. That was after Ala had gone, and we had the responsibility. The girls did what they could, but, of course, they had their own families by then, except Nellie, and she wouldn't come to see him if any of the others were coming.

It wouldn't be held a disgrace, now—certainly not. The kids pray to go into the movies—and isn't that the same? But we held it a disgrace to us. I guess Nellie was my favorite sister—she took more after the uncles than the rest of us. She wasn't pretty, exactly, but she had a black-haired imp in her, and she was the first to marry of all the girls. I can see her face under the bridal veil, looking frightened. That's funny for Nellie O'Mara, the Wild Irish Rose. O'Mara was my grandda's name—she took it when she ran off with her piano pounder and started showing her legs on the public stage. The old man, queer enough, didn't mind so much—he had European ideas about the theatre. But Ma was horrified and so were the other girls.

I was horrified myself—I had to fight three boys on account of it. And Nellie's husband, Ed Meany, would come around and sit on the stoop, looking as if he'd just had a tooth pulled and telling all he'd done for Nellie, and how, even now, he'd been willing to take her back. He was a good man, no doubt, but he talked till you'd feel like shooting him. It wasn't till I had my own trouble that I knew how he felt.

The other girls married all right and respectable,—Grace and Kathleen,—though I never did think much of Carl Schuhmacher. He always looked too much like one of his own sirloin steaks, but that was Grace's affair, not mine, and the meat market's a good business. We thought she could have done better for herself, but I don't know, as things turned out. He had some trouble, during the war, till young Carl was killed at Cantigny. I guess he's forgotten the trouble—I don't mean forgotten young Carl. They've still got the picture in the parlor, and the uniform looks queer, now. But he and John Pollard—that's Kathy's husband—get on a lot better than they did. There was feeling between the two families for a long time, over the meat-carving set and the Irish lace doilies. Well, Grace was always a grabber, and she did her best to make John Pollard feel small. But he got to be principal of Van Twiller for six months before they retired him—and I've seen his office. He was the steady sort that works up, and they couldn't keep him out of the position, though they tried. Now he's got the testimonial framed and it means something to him. I know that by the way he looks at it, now and then. Their youngest's teaching at Hunter, and they make a lot of that.

II

I can't say I've had a bad life, though it hasn't been quite what 1 expected. If I'd gone in with Uncle Martin—he was always the clever one! And I was his favorite, in a manner of speaking. But I couldn't stand the bother of politics—not even when he got to be district leader. He might have gone far, I think, but he picked the wrong side, in the Hall. That's the unforgivable mistake. Then, later on, he had his trouble—well, the jury disagreed at both trials. But it was all over the papers, and that sticks to a man. My clever, low-spoken uncle! I remember him always, a little disdainful of the rest of them, and you felt he took a drink to be friendly, and yet not to be really friendly. And then, at the trial, he was an old man, with jowls and white hair, answering just as clever and low-spoken as he always had, and yet not making a good impression. Because times had changed—that was all—and yet, how would he have done different? It was in his blood to rise by any means he could lay hands on, and pull up his family, too. But I'm glad that it didn't interest me—though he helped me get my first position.

Well, now, I was young and strong, though you might not think it. I wanted to go on the Force—but then the job came along. My old man wanted me to follow in his own line of business. But I didn't feel like messing around all day with little wheels and springs and an eyeglass stuck in one eye. They were building the Subway in those days—well, that's how I started. It was good pay, for the time, and I wanted to marry Eileen.

It's queer what a man's work in life will turn out to be. You go around the top of the city—well, I know that, too. But it's underneath where I've worked, the strong part of my life. You don't often get to thinking of it—a man's work is his work, wherever it lies. But, if it wasn't for thousands of men whose names you've never heard of, all living their lives underground, it wouldn't be a city, or the same city. I'd think of it, now and again, on the night shift, when things got quiet above. They'd have gone to sleep by then,—yes, even the rich and proud,—but we'd be working. It's hard to put to you so you'll understand it. You see the place in the street where it's planked over, and the taxi has to slow up, and you start to swear. But, underneath, there's the work gangs, and the lights.

It gives you a pride, in a way, to be part of it—at least, at times. You feel as if the people just walking the streets were different people and didn't know. It's hard for me to explain that—I don't know the way to say it. But I'm glad I did what I did—if it did mean ending up in a change booth, and then the pension. It does for Martha and me.

Eileen always expected more of me, and maybe she was right to do so. But a young man, in his strength, that's bossing a gang—well, that's all a young man might like. He could well be wrong about it, but he'd have to be shown where he was wrong. But, when I found out what was happening, I broke every stick of furniture in the flat. 1 did so. She wasn't afraid of me, either—I'd have killed her if she had been. But she stood there, cold and proud, with the look she'd had when I first saw her, the look of a woman untouched. He'd come as a boarder because we had the extra room that wasn't needed for the baby after all a—whey-faced, shrewd little man. I wasn't as angry at him, for some queer reason—I think he did his best to be decent, through it all. But she was ambitious, always, and we had no children.

Well, he made the money—he made a great deal before he died. Mrs. Loring Masters and the big house on Long Island and the children sent to fine colleges, except for the one that killed himself. When the daughter was married, I saw the picture in the paper, and she had just the look of Eileen. I wished her no ill—I wished her great good fortune. I wished her mother no ill—yet I wondered if the man had really touched her, after all. There were times when we lay beside each other, in our youth, and asked no better. I know that, for that is not something a man forgets. And it was the same with her. But she wanted other than that.

I don't know how to tell it all—I wish I knew. How am I to tell what it's like to come home, to the quiet street, after the night shift, with nothing but the milkman's horse clopping his way along—and be tired to bone and marrow and yet satisfied?

How am I to tell what it's like, day after day? The city stretches and you don't notice it, till one day you go to the Park, and the buildings have grown up like a fence around it. I remember talking to my Uncle Matthew. He'd had thirty-five years on the Force and retired as inspector, and he should know if anyone did. Well, he talked about many changes, in an old man's voice, and how there was still as much law in the end of a night stick as in many law books. But he didn't really touch it.

It reminds me of the one time I went to Proctor's when Nellie was on the bill. She did well, and I was shamed to the bone, but I couldn't help applauding. The audience liked her, too—they knew she came from Third Avenue and was one of their own. I've given her change at the window, since, and she didn't know me. Nobody ever looks at the man in the change booth—nobody knows if he has a face. Why should I be worried about that? Well, I'm not, to tell you the truth. But it's given me a chuckle, now and then, when somebody's come along and said, "Why, Ed!"

Have I given you any idea? Most likely not. I've seen Teddy Roosevelt, the young dude back from the war, and his teeth were just the way they are in the pictures. I've shook hands with John McGraw—and seen the sudden, white, Irish rage on his face when somebody yelled "Muggsy" at him out of the crowd. I've seen the Mayor, by the Zoo, showing his boy the polar bears—and him in his queer black hat and people leaving him alone. But where do you begin and end? I remember John Pollard, that's educated, telling me once about some city in Europe where you dug down and under the city was the ruins of another city and under that ruin another till you could not come to the end of them. Now that's something any New Yorker could understand. It's Jimmy Walker's town and Rabbi Wise's, it's LaGuardia's and J. P. Morgan's and Cardinal Spellman's, and the new strong hitter on the Yankees' and Katharine Cornell's. It belongs to the telephone repairmen and the Park Avenue dolls, to the fellow that peddles the racing sheets and the choirboys in the Cathedral and all the hackers in their cabs. Now how would I say whose town it was, precisely? Yet I'd like to know.

Well, now, there was my friend Louis Jordan, went into domestic service. It didn't seem work for a man to me, at first, and yet I liked him well. I ran into him first at Joe's place, the summer that Eileen had left me—a very dignified creature, though drink was his weakness. But you could neither smell it nor see it on him—at least at that time. The rich man he worked for had closed his house for the summer and left Louis and his wife the caretaking of it. A dignified creature, I say, with soft, puffy hands and a face not far off a priest's. His wife was a little thin woman, most respectable, in black. But, when he got to know me well, he'd ask me back for a nip, now and then, at the house. Man, dear, you never saw a kitchen stove to equal that one—it could have roasted an ox. Then we'd have our nip and his wife would run the cards for me, very considerate and respectable, for she knew I'd had troubles. And all around us and over us was the big, grand, stately house with its pictures and its fine furniture, and yet we the only things alive in it, like mice in a cheese.

He took me through the whole of it, one warm Sunday afternoon. There was a bathtub of marble, though it looked like dusty stone, and the man of the house had twenty suits left in his closet, and yet he had others, for he'd not appear naked where he was. It gave me a queer feeling to see all those suits, hanging up on their hangers. Then, when we got back to the kitchen, we found that Mrs. Jordan had got hold of the gin bottle and was stretched out, highly respectable but stiff as a corpse, on the floor. So, after that, I knew his sorrow, as he had known mine. Yet, the next winter, I happened to pass by the house. There was a red carpet down and all the fine carriages drawing up at the door. And, just as the door opened, I saw Louis Jordan, like a sentinel on post in his dress suit, receiving them all, with the young men to help him. Very fine he looked, and not like the man with his collar off that I'd drunk with, in the kitchen. And she, no doubt, was helping equally, with the ladies. Well, that's a long time ago, and the house is gone.

III

I've seen some queer sights, I have. I've stuck my head up from a manhole and seen six elephants, marching down Eighth Avenue, holding on to each other's tails. It was only for the circus in Madison Square Garden, but it gave you a turn. Then there was the bar the midgets used to frequent. I don't remember the name of it, but I stumbled in there one night and thought I'd gone mad when all the little faces turned at me. I've seen other things as well. I've seen them shower the ticker tape and the torn paper from the high buildings and got a glimpse of the face of the man they were welcoming. It might be one face or another, but it looked white and dazzled. And next week you'd have forgotten his name.

I used to go to the ball games often, with Martha, and that's a sight, too, when the game goes into extra innings and the crowd sits tight and the shadow begins to grow on the infield. Her brother was with the Giants, for a year—Swede Nansen, they called him—a tall, blond, slow-spoken boy. He could pitch with the best, on his day, but he liked farming better, which is a queer thing in a man. I remember the time he struck out nine Cubs in five innings, and the yelling of the crowd. But the next year his arm went bad on him and nothing could be done for it. He played for Atlanta a while,—the South being recommended for him,—then he gave up the game and settled down to his farming, and now, every Christmas, he sends us a box of pecans. But his record's still in the books, and the game where he beat Alexander. I should like to see him again, for he was a man I respected, but I doubt now that I will.

She's been a good wife to me, Martha, and never ashamed of a man that worked with his hands—though I do not do so any more. At one time we had the money, and that was a contrary experience. She was left five hundred dollars, and that sharp little fellow, Abe Leavis, told us what to buy. At first I felt queer, going into the grand office, but soon I saw my money was as good as another's. Yet, though I will not criticize any other man's work, it does not seem to me a man's occupation to do nothing but watch the figures change on a blackboard. They thought, for a while, that I was lucky, for those days had no sense to them at all. And indeed, I thought so myself. I've had men in their handmade suits ask me for advice, and take it, too. They'd have taken advice, at that time, from a horse, if the horse was winning on the market. Well, it was forty thousand dollars before it was nothing—so you can say that I've had the experience of riches. It takes a man's mind off his work—that's all I can say. But we had the sealskin coat for Martha and the washing machine.

If I told you about Abe Leavis, that would be part of it, too. That was a rubber ball of a man, a rubber ball bounced up and down the pavements. I have seen him so thin and pitiful it would break your heart; I have seen him round and plump, with his pockets full of cigars. You could kill that man, but you could not put him down. But how he loved the smell and taste of the city! I'll forgive a man much for that. No, it wasn't my city he loved—it was Fifth and Park and the riches—the big shining toy- store where everything's for sale. It was like a tonic to him to pay maybe twenty dollars for a pair of theatre tickets and get there late for the play. But that's part of it, too.

Now there's whole sections and locations I've never seen. It wasn't so long ago that I visited my grandnephew, Francis. He married a Jewish girl when he'd finished his internship—a pretty, bright young thing—and they've got an apartment on the Grand Concourse. I walked twenty blocks after I'd left them and it was like another city. And yet it couldn't have been any other city. It couldn't have been.

I don't know if it's the two rivers make it—though I knew the captain of the *Michael T. McQuillan,* and a good man he was and told me the work there is to get the big, proud liners into dock. I don't know if it's the climate that makes it—the fine fall and the dirty winter, the hot summer and the spring that comes with the flower carts and touches your heart. It's a healthy climate, I've always thought, though others may differ. Now when Martha and I were first married we'd go as far as Far Rockaway for a bite of the summer. And that was a change and healthy—but I noticed we were glad to get back where you knew the look of the streets. I don't know—I couldn't say—it's hard for me to tell.

Well, now, there's the being old. But we got along very comfortable. There's a lot of them move away—to Florida, let's say—and then they send you the postcards, saying what a fine time they're having. No doubt they are, if they like it, but I never could see it made them look any younger. There was my friend, the Dutchman, that retired from his delicatessen and went to live with his granddaughter at White Plains. It was a nice house, to be sure, and he kept the lawn very well cut. I congratulated him on that. Then he looked at me and there was a grief in his eyes. "Vy, Ed," he said, "it's all right. But you can't cut the lawn all day. I tell you, some nights, I vake up and listen for the noise of the El. And, ven it ain't there, I feel old. Ed, I'd give ten dollars if Mrs. Burke was to come in—the fussy one—just to tell me she vouldn't put up with this kind of service no more."

Then his granddaughter came to tell him it was time for his nap, and, though she was very polite, I knew I should go away. Thank God, I've been spared that—though we've neither chick nor child.

It's cool enough in the flat, and if there's a breeze we get it. And there's always something to look at—the boys playing ball in the streets, shouting under the light, summer evenings, and the taxis drawing up to the apartment house opposite, and a young woman coming out, with bare arms. Phil Kelly, the doorman there, is a friend of mine, though he comes from Ulster. They'd be surprised, in that house, if they knew the things that I know about them. I don't mean any ugly things—just the odd little circumstances. It's my hope that the pretty dark girl will marry the young man with glasses. He's steadier than the one that's bet-ter-dressed. I'd like to tell her that, only how would I tell her?

There isn't a trace or a place of my childhood's house. There isn't a trace or a place of the house where I lived with Eileen. Now last year, when I went to the cemetery, it took me an hour to find Uncle Martin's grave, though they'd kept it decent, and he was a well-known man.

You'd think such a thing might make you sad, but again, it does not. It's comfortable, in a way, to be like the dust in the air. It's hard for me to tell it, and yet, what I mean is this. Last summer I went to the Fair, and that's a great sight, no doubt of it. Oh, the crowds and the proud buildings of the nations of the earth and the horns tooting "All around the town"!

It was some State Day when we went there, and there was the Governor of the State, with the sirens blowing in front of him to clear the way. Well, I wouldn't remember which State it was, but that makes little difference. There were all the top hats there to receive him, and that's only courtesy. And yet he was swal-lowed up in the Fair itself, and, except for the people from his own State, there was no one knew he was there, or cared at all. So it came upon me, that day—sitting on a bench, with my feet tired—it all came upon me. For they all seemed to pass by me, the rich and the great and the proud, with the sirens blowing in front of them. And yet, that wasn't the city, and when the Fair itself was finished, there'd be many still in the city that hadn't even seen it. It was a fine sight to see, but they hadn't missed it, in their lives.

And so it was with the most of us—and with the city itself. For it wasn't the mayors and the millionaires and the Presidents—though I've walked by the President's house and seen him go in. It was my Uncle Ally and my Uncle Matthew, my friend Louis Jordan and my sister, Nellie O'Mara, the boys that were on the gang with me and the boys that died underground. It's the small, new honeymoon couples, buying a coffee ring at the corner bakery, and the guards who walk the museums, clean and pudgy; the thieves in the morning round-up and the good men, like my old man, who live and die without notice. It's all that, and the moon at the end of the street where you never expected a moon.

I said, "Martha, I'm tired, I think," and she took me home. So next day, when I was no better, she called my grandnephew, Francis. He's been very kind, and, where some might be afraid of the hospital, I am not. It's a good, sunny room, the ward, and the nurses very attentive to an old man. From where I lie on my back, I can see the river.

So, since it's to be that way, I'm glad it's to be that way. Wouldn't I have been the fool to go to a place like White Plains and die there? A man could hardly die easy in those foreign places—a man who's seen what I've seen. I'm aware there are other cities. The day orderly comes from London, and we've talked about that one.

I was born in Brooklyn, but we moved to the East Side, afterwards. I remember my mother's baking bread, and the Empire State, when it was new. You won't remember Swede Nansen, though his record's in the book, but I remember him. You won't remember Martin O'Mara, but he was part of it. You won't remember Logan's on Fourteenth Street, but it was a fine, large store.

When they bomb the town to pieces, with their planes from the sky, there'll be a big ghost left. When it's gone, they'd better let the sea come in and cover it, for there never will be one like it in the ages of man again.

GLAMOUR

(1932)

I USED TO READ quite a lot of books when I was younger, but now they just make me sore. Marian keeps on bringing them back from the lending library and, occasionally, I'll pick one up and read a few chapters, but sooner or later you're bound to strike something that makes you sick. I don't mean dirt or anything—just foolishness, and people acting the way they never act. Of course, the books she reads are mostly love stories. I suppose they're the worst kind.

But what I understand least is the money angle. It takes money to get drunk and it takes money to go around with a girl—at least that's been my experience. But the people in those books seem to have invented a special kind of money—it only gets spent on a party or a trip. The rest of the time they might as well be paying their bills with wampum, as far as you can figure it out.

Of course, often enough, the people in books are poor. But then they're so darn poor, it's crazy. And, often enough, just when everything's at its worst, some handy little legacy comes and the new life opens out before them right away, like a great big tulip. Well, I only had one legacy in my life and I know what I did with that. It darn near ruined me.

Uncle Bannard died up in Vermont in 1924, and when his estate was settled, it came to $1237.62 apiece for Lou and me.—Lou's husband put her share in Greater Los Angeles real estate—they live out on the Coast—and I guess they've done pretty well. But I took mine and quit the firm I was with, Rosenberg and Jenkins, mechanical toys and novelties, and went to Brooklyn to write a novel.

It sounds crazy, looking back on it. But I was a bug about reading and writing in those days, and I'd done some advertising copy for the firm that pulled. And that was the time when everybody was getting steamed up about "the new American writers," and it looked like a game without much overhead. I'd just missed the war—I was seventeen when it finished—and I'd missed college because of father's death. In fact, I hadn't done much of anything I really wanted since I had to quit high school—though the novelty business was all right as businesses go. So when I got a chance to cut loose, I cut.

I figured I could easily live a year on the twelve hundred, and, at first, I thought of France. But there'd be the nuisance of learning frog-talk and the passage there and back. Besides, I wanted to be near a big library. My novel was going to be about the American Revolution, if you can picture it. I'd read "Henry Esmond" over and over and I wanted to write a book like that.

I guess it must have been a bunch of my New England ancestors that picked Brooklyn for me. They were pioneers, all right—but, gosh, how they hated to take any chance but a big one! And I'm like that myself. I like to feel tidy in my mind when I'm taking a chance.

I figured I could be as solitary in Brooklyn as I could in Pisa, and a lot more comfortable. I knew how many words it took to make a novel—I'd counted some of them—so I bought enough paper and a second-hand typewriter and pencils and erasers. That about cleaned out my ready cash. I swore I wouldn't touch the legacy till I was really at work. But I felt like a million dollars—I swear I felt as if I were looking for treasure—when I got into the subway that shiny autumn day, and started across the river to look for a room.

It may have been my ancestors that sent me to Brooklyn, but I don't know what landed me at Mrs. Forge's. Old Wrestling Southgate, the one who was bothered with witches, would probably have called it a flowered snare of the fiend. And I'm not so sure, looking back, that he'd have been wrong.

Mrs. Forge opened the door herself—Serena was out. They'd talked about putting an ad in the paper but they'd just never got around to it; and, naturally, they wouldn't have put up a card. If it hadn't looked like the sort of house I'd wanted, I'd never have rung the bell. As it was, when she came to the door, I thought that I had made a mistake. So the first thing I did was beg her pardon.

She had on her black silk dress—the one with the white ruffles—just as if she were going out calling in the barouche. The minute she started to speak, I knew she was Southern. They all had that voice. I won't try to describe it. There's nothing worse than a whiny one—it beats the New England twang. But theirs didn't whine. They made you think of the sun and long afternoons and slow rivers—and time, time, time, just sliding along like a current, not going anywhere particular, but gay.

I think she liked my begging her pardon, for she took me in and gave me a slice of fruit cake and some lemonade. And I listened to her talk and felt, somehow, as if I'd been frozen for a long time and was just beginning to get warm. There was always a pitcher of lemonade in the ice-box, though the girls drank "coke," mostly. I've seen them come in from the snow, in the dead of winter, and drink it. They didn't think much of the cold, anyway, so they more or less pretended it didn't exist. They were that way.

The room was exactly what I wanted—big and sunny, with an outlook over a little backyard where there was the wreck of a forsythia bush and some spindly grass. I've forgotten to say the house was in one of those old-fashioned side-streets, not far from Prospect Park. But it doesn't matter where it was. It must be gone, now.

You know, it took all my nerve to ask Mrs. Forge the price. She was very polite, but she made me feel like a guest. I don't know if you can understand that. And then she couldn't tell me.

"Well, now, Mr. Southgate," she said, in that soft, gentle, helpless voice that ran on as inexorably as water, "I wish my daughter Eva had been here to receive you. My daughter Eva has accepted a business position since we came here for my daughter Melissa's art training. And I said, only this morning, 'Eva, honey, suppose Serena's away and some young person comes here, askin' for that room. I'll be bound to say somethin' to them, sugar, and I'll feel right embarrassed.' But just then some little boys started shoutin' down the street and I never did rightly hear what she answered. So if you're in a hurry, Mr. Southgate, I don't just know what we can do."

"I could leave a deposit," I said. I'd noticed, by this time, that the black silk had a tear in it and that she was wearing a pair of run-down ball-slippers—incredibly small they were. But, all the same, she looked like a duchess.

"Why, I suppose you could, Mr. Southgate," she said, with an obvious lack of interest. "I suppose that would be businesslike. You gentlemen in the North are always so interested in business. I recollect Mr. Forge sayin' before he died, 'Call them d— Yankees if you like, Milly, but we've all got to live in the same country and I've met some without horns.' Mr. Forge was always so humorous. So, you see, we're quite accustomed to Northerners.

You don't happen to be kin to the Mobile Southgates, do you, Mr. Southgate? You'll excuse an old lady's askin'—but you seem to favor them a little, now your face is in the light."

I'm not trying to put down just the way she talked—she didn't say "ah" and "nah"—it was something lighter and suaver. But her talk went on like that. They all did it. It wasn't nervousness or trying to impress you. They found it as easy and restful to talk as most of us do to keep still; and, if the talk never got anywhere, they'd never expected it would. It was like a drug—it made life into a dream. And, of course, it isn't that.

Finally, I simply went for my stuff and moved in. I didn't know how much I was paying or what meals would be included in it, but I somehow felt that these things would be shown unto me when the time was ripe. That's what an hour and a half with Mrs. Forge did to me. But I did resolve to have a clear understanding with "my daughter, Eva," who seemed to be the business head of the family.

Serena let me in when I came back. I gave her fifty cents to get in her good graces and she took an instant dislike to me which never wavered. She was small and black and withered, with bright little sparks of eyes. I don't know how long she'd been with them, but I thought of her growing on the family, like mistletoe, from immemorial time.

Whenever I heard her singing in the kitchen, I felt as if she were putting a private curse on me. "Honey-bird—" she'd croon—"honey-bird, no one gwine tuh fly away wid mah honey-bird. Ole buzzard, he try his wings—he flap and he flap—man wid a gun he see him—hi, hi, hi—shoot ole buzzard wid a buckshot and never tetch mah honey-bird."

I knew who the old buzzard was, all right. And it may sound funny—but it wasn't. It was spooky. Eva wouldn't see it; they'd all treat Serena like a combination of unavoidable nuisance and troublesome child. I don't understand how they can treat servants that way. I mean friendly and grand at the same time. It isn't natural.

It sounds as if I were trying to keep from telling about Eva. I don't know why I'm doing that.

I got unpacked and pretty well settled. My room was on the third floor, back, but I could hear the girls coming home. There'd be the door and steps and a voice saying, "Honey, I'm so tired—I'm just plumb dragged out," and Mrs. Forge saying, "Now, honey, you rest yourself." There were three of those. I kind of wondered why they were all so tired. Later on, I found that was just something they said.

But then Mrs. Forge would begin to talk and they wouldn't be tired any more. They'd be quite excited and there'd be a good deal of laughter. I began to feel very uncomfortable. And then I got stubborn. After all, I'd rented the room.

So, when Eva finally knocked at the door, I just grunted, "Come in!" the way you would to a chamber-maid. She opened the door and stood in the doorway, hesitant. I imagine Melissa had bet her she wouldn't have the nerve.

"Mr. Southgate, I believe?" she said, quite vaguely, as if I might be anything from a cloud to a chest of drawers.

"Dr. Livingstone, I presume?" I said. There was an old picture on the wall—the two Englishmen meeting formally in the middle of a paper jungle. But I'll hand her something—she saw I wasn't trying to be fresh.

"I reckon we have been making a lot of racket," she said. "But that's mostly Melissa. She never was rightly raised. Won't you give us the favor of your company downstairs, Mr. Southgate? We-all don't act crazy. We just sound like it."

She was dark, you know, and yet she had that white skin. There's a kind of flower called freesia—when the petals are very white, they have the color of her skin. And there's a strong sweetness to it—strong and ghostly at the same time. It smells like spring with the ghosts in it, between afternoon and dusk. And there's a word they call glamour. It was there.

She had small white teeth and red lips. There was one little freckle in the hollow of her throat—I don't know how she happened to have only one. Louisa was the beauty and Melissa the artist. They'd settled it that way. I couldn't have fallen in love with Louisa or Melissa. And yet, I liked to see them all together—the three sisters—I'd liked to have lived in a big, cool house by a river and spent my life seeing them all together. What fool thoughts you get, when you're young! I'd be the Northern cousin who managed the place. I used to send myself to sleep with it, every night, for months.

Mrs. Forge wasn't in it, or Serena. It was a big place—it went on for miles and miles. Most of the land wasn't good for much and the Negroes were bone-lazy, but I made them work. I'd get up in the first mist of morning and be in the saddle all day, overseeing and planning. But, always, I'd be coming back, on a tired horse, up that flowery avenue and they'd be waiting for me on the porch, the three white dresses bunched like a bouquet.

They'd be nice to me, because I was weary, and I'd go upstairs to the room looking over the river and change out of my hot clothes and wash. Then Eva would send me up a long drink with mint in it and I'd take it slowly. After supper, when I wasn't doing accounts, they'd sing or we'd all play some foolish sort of round game with ivory counters. I guess I got most of it out of books, but it was very real to me. That's one trouble with books—you get things out of them.

Often we got old, but it never seemed to change us much. Once in a while the other girls were married and, sometimes, I married Eva, But we never had any children and none of us ever moved away. I kept on working like a dog and they accepted it and I was content. We had quite a few neighbors, at first, but I got tired of that. So I made it a river island you could only reach by boat, and that was more satisfactory.

It wasn't a dream, you know, or anything sappy like that. I just made it up in my head. Toward the end of the year, I'd lie awake for hours, making it up, but it never seemed to tire me. I never really told Eva about it at all, not even when we were engaged. Maybe it would have made a difference, but I don't think so.

She wasn't the kind of person you'd tell any dreams to. She was in the dream. I don't mean she was noble or fatal or like a ghost. I've had her in my arms and she was warm and alive and you could have had children by her, because things are that way. But that wasn't the point—that wasn't the point at all.

She didn't even have much imagination. None of them had. They just lived, like trees. They didn't plan or foresee. I've spent hours trying to explain to Mrs. Forge that, if you had ten dollars, it wasn't just ten dollars, it was something you could put in a savings bank. She'd listen, very politely. But ten dollars, to her, was just something that went away. They thought it was fine if you had money, but they thought it was equally fine if you had a good-looking nose. Money was rather like rain to them—it fell or it didn't—and, they knew that there wasn't any way to make it rain.

I'm sure they'd never have come North at all, if it hadn't been for some obscure family dispute. They often seemed to wonder about it themselves. And I heard the dispute talked about dozens of times but I never really got the gist of it, except that it was connected with two things, the new spur-track to the turpentine plant, and Cousin Belle. "Cousin Belle, she just acted so mean—she gave up her manners," Mrs. Forge would say, placidly. "She left us no reco'se, Bannard—no reco'se at all." And then the girls would chime in. I suppose they got the money to come North from selling land to the turpentine plant, but even of that I am not sure.

Anyhow, they had golden visions, as they would have. Louisa was going to be a great actress and Melissa a great artist—and Eva—I don't know exactly what Eva expected, even now. But it was something. And it was all going to happen without any real work, it was going to fall from a cloud. Oh, yes, Melissa and Louisa went to classes and Eva had a job, but those, you felt, were stopgaps. They were passing the time till the cloud opened and the manna fell.

I'll say this for them—it didn't seem to hurt them to have their visions fail. The only person it really hurt was me.

Because I believed them, at first. How could I help it? The dream I had wasn't so wrong. They were living on an island—an island in the middle of Brooklyn—a piece of where they came from. People came to the house—art students and such—there were always plenty of young men. But, once inside the house, they submitted to the house. Serena would pass the cold ham, at supper, and you'd look out of the window and be surprised to find it snowing, for the window should have been open and the warm night coming through. I don't know what roomers they'd ever had before, but in my time there was only myself and Mr. Budd. He was a fat little clerk of fifty, very respectable, and he stayed because of the food, for Serena was a magnificent, wasteful cook.

Yes, I believed it, I believed in it all. It was like an enchantment. It was glamour. I believed in all they said and I saw them all going back to Chantry—the three famous sisters with their three distinguished husbands—like people in a fairy-tale.

We'd all have breakfast together, but the only person who talked much then was Mr. Budd. The Forges never were properly alive till later in the day. At breakfast, you saw them through a veil. Sometimes I'd feel my heart beat, staring at Eva, because she looked like one of those shut flowers in greenhouses—something shut and mysterious so you fairly held your breath, waiting for it to open. I suppose it was just because she took a long time to wake up.

Then Mr. Budd and the girls would go away, and, when my bed was made, I'd go up and work. I'm not saying much about the novel, but I worked hard on it. I'd made a little chart on cardboard with 365 squares and each day I'd ink one in.

I'd go out for lunch and take a walk afterwards. A man has to have regular exercise, and that's free. Then I'd work some more, until they started to come home. I couldn't work after that—not after the first months. But I'd make myself not listen for Eva's step.

The first time I kissed Eva was the New Year's party. One of Louisa's beaus had brought some red wine and we were singing and fooling around. Serena was off for the evening and Eva and I were out in the kitchen, looking for clean glasses. We were both feeling gay and it just seemed natural. I didn't even think of it again till the next afternoon, when we'd all gone to the movies. And then I suddenly began to shake all over, as if I had a chill, remembering, and she said, "What is it, honey?" and her hand slipped into my hand.

That was how it began. And that night I started inventing the river plantation. And I'm not a fool and I've been around. But I held hands with that girl through January, February, and most of March before I really kissed her again. I can't explain it at all. She wasn't being coy or mean or trying to fight me. It was as if we were floating downstream in a boat together, and it was so pleasant to look at her and be near her, you didn't need any more. The pain hadn't started, then.

And yet, all through that time, something in me was fighting, fighting, to get out of the boat, to get away from the river. It wasn't my river at all, you know. It never was. And part of me knew it. But, when you're in love, you haven't got common sense.

By the end of March, the novel was more than half finished. I'd allowed two months for revision and making contacts, which seemed sensible. And, one evening, it was cold, and Eva and I took a walk in the park. And when we came in, Mrs. Forge made us some hot cocoa—the other girls had gone to bed early, for once—and, while we were drinking it, Mrs. Forge fell asleep in her chair. And we put down our cups, as if it were a signal, and kissed—and the house was very quiet and we could hear her breathing, like sleep itself, through the long kiss.

Next morning, I woke up and the air felt warm and, when I looked out in the yard, there were leaves on the forsythia bush. Eva was just the same at breakfast, shut and mysterious, and I was just the same. But, when I went up to work, I shook my fist at old Wrestling Southgate, the fellow that was bothered with witches. Because I was going to marry Eva, and he could go to grass.

I tell you, they didn't plan or foresee. I told Mrs. Forge very straight just how I stood—finances and everything—and they treated it like a party. They were all as kind and excited as they could be, except Serena. She just refused to believe it and sang a lot more about buzzards. And, somehow or other, that made me feel queerer than ever. Because I knew Serena hated me but I knew she was a real person. I could understand her, she was close to the ground. And I loved the others but I didn't understand them, and sometimes I wouldn't be sure they were quite real. It was that way with Eva, even though we were in love.

I could kiss her but I couldn't be sure that she was always there when I kissed her. It wasn't coldness, it was merely another climate. I could talk for hours about what we were going to do when we were married and every time I stopped she'd say, "Go on, honey, it makes me feel so nice to hear you talk." But she'd have been as pleased if I'd sung it instead. God knows I didn't expect her to understand the novelty business, or even writing. But, sometimes, I'd honestly feel as if we didn't speak the same language. Which was foolish, because she wasn't foreign.

I remember getting angry with her one evening because I found out she was still writing to this boy friend, down South, and hadn't even told him about Us. She opened her eyes very wide.

"Why, honey," she said, in the most reasonable of voices, "I couldn't stop writing Furfew right off like that. I've just always been sort of engaged to Furfew."

"Well, now you're engaged to me," I said.

"I know," she said. "That's why I can't stop writing him, honey. It would hurt Furfew something dreadful if he knew I had to stop writing him because I was engaged to you."

"Look here," I said, wondering which of us was crazy, "are we going to be married?"

"Of co'se, honey."

"Then what," I said, "has this Furfew got to do with it? Are you engaged to him or me?"

"Of co'se I'm engaged to you, honey, and we're going to get married. But Furfew, he's kind of like kin, and we been engaged a long time. It seems right mean and uncivil to break off with him short like that."

"I don't believe it," I said, "I don't believe there are any Furfews. It sounds like something you grow under glass. What's he like?"

She thought for a long time.

"He's right cute," she said finally. "But he's got a little doin's of a black moustache."

I managed to find out, however, that he owned the turpentine plant and was considered quite the John D. Rockefeller of Chantry. I was so used to no one in Chantry ever having any money that was worth anything, that this came as an unpleasing surprise. After that, Furfew used to try to come to the river plantation in a very shiny motor-launch with a red-and-white awning and I would warn him off with a shotgun.

But then the money business began. You like to give a girl presents when you're in love—you like to do things right. Well, Lord knows, Eva was no gold-digger—she was as likely to be pleased with a soda as a pair of imported gloves. On the other hand, she was as likely to be pleased with the gloves.

I kept on schedule with the work, but I couldn't with the money. Each week, I'd be just a little over the line. I tell you, the people in books don't know about money. The people who write them can tell what it's like to be broke. But they don't tell what it's like to go around with clothes enough to cover you and food enough to satisfy you, and still have your heart's desire depend on money you haven't got.

Sure, I could have gone back in the novelty business and Eva could have kept on working. That would have been right for nine people out of ten. But it wouldn't have been right for the way I felt about Eva. It can be like that.

I wanted to come to her—oh, like a rescuer, I suppose. Like a prince, like the Northern cousin that saved the plantation. I didn't want to make the best of things—I wanted it all. You can't compromise with glamour. Or that's the way I feel.

Besides, I'd put in eight months' work on that novel and it didn't seem sensible to throw it all away. It might be a ladder to climb out on. It might have been.

Eva never complained, but she never understood. She'd just say we could all go back and live in Chantry. Well, I'm not that kind of man. If it had only been the river plantation! But, by now, I knew Chantry as well as if I'd been born there, and there wasn't a thing for me to do. Except maybe a job in Furfew's turpentine plant. And wouldn't that have been pretty?

Then, gradually, I got to know that the Forges, too, were almost at the end of their string. I had to get it casually they never talked about those things directly. But when you keep on spending what you've got, there comes a time when you don't have it any more. Only, it always surprised them. I wish I was built that way.

It was the middle of July by this time, and one Saturday afternoon Eva came home and said she'd been let off at her office. They were cutting down the staff. I'd just been going over my accounts, and when she told me that, I started laughing as if I couldn't stop.

She looked rather surprised at first, but then she laughed, too. "Why, honey," she said, "you're the killin'est. You always take things so serious. And then, sometimes, you don't take them serious a bit."

"It's an old Northern custom," I said. "They call it 'Laugh, clown, laugh.' For God's sake, Eva, what are we going to do?" "Why, honey," she said, "I suppose I could get me another position." She never told me it was up to me. She never would have. "But I just sort of despise those mean old offices. Do you think I ought to get me another position, honey?"

"Oh, darling, it doesn't matter," I said, still laughing. "Nothing matters but us."

"That's mighty sweet of you, honey," she said and she looked relieved. "That's just the way I feel. And, when we get married, we'll fix things up right nice for Melissa and Louisa, won't we?

And mother, of co'se, because she just can't stand Cousin Belle."
"Sure," I said. "Sure. When we're married, we'll fix up everything." And we went out in the back yard to look at the forsythia
bush. But that night, Furfew brought his launch inshore and
landed on the lower end of the island. He pitched camp there,
and I could see his fire at night, through a glass.

I can't describe the next two months very well. They were
all mixed up, the reality and the dream. Alelissa and Louisa had
to give up their classes, so we were all home, and lots of people
came to the house. Some of them were callers and some of them
were bill-collectors but, whoever they were, they generally stayed
to a meal. Serena never minded that, she liked company. I remember paying a grocery bill, with almost the last of my legacy,
toward the end. There were eight hams on the bill and ten cases
of "coke." It hadn't been paid for a long time.

Often, we'd all pile into an old Ford that belonged to one of
the art students and go down to a public beach for the day. Eva
didn't care so much about swimming but she loved to lie in the
sand. And I'd lie beside her, painfully happy, and we'd hardly
say anything at all. My God, but she was beautiful against those
beach colors—the clear greens of the water and the hot white
and tan of the sand. But then, she was just as beautiful, sitting in
the plush rocker in the front parlor, under that green lamp.

They say the time between the Ordinance of Secession and
the firing on Sumter was one of the gayest seasons Charleston
ever had. I can understand that. They'd come to the brink of
something, and fate was out of their hands. I got to feel that
way.

Everything mixed, I tell you, everything mixed. I'd be sitting on the beach with Eva and, at the same time, I'd be riding
around the river plantation, getting reports from my foreman
and planning years ahead. I got to love that place. Even toward

the end, it was safe, it didn't change. Of course, we kept having more and more trouble with Furfew; he kept extending his lines from the lower end of the island, but it never came to actual warfare—just fights between our men.

Meanwhile, I finished the novel and started revising it. And sometimes Eva would say why didn't we get married, anyway, and I knew we couldn't. You can't get married without some future ahead of you. So we started having arguments, and that was bad.

Why didn't I just seduce her like the big, brave heroes in books? Well, there were times when I thought it might be the answer for both of us. But it never happened. It wasn't shame or good principles. It just isn't so awfully easy to seduce a dream.

I knew they were writing letters but I didn't want to know any more. I knew the legacy was gone and my savings account was going, but I didn't care. I just wanted things to go on.

Finally, I heard that Furfew was coming North. I was going around like a sleepwalker most of the time, then, so it didn't hit me, at first. And then it did hit me.

Eva and I were out in the back yard. We'd fixed up an old swing seat there and it was dusky. Serena was humming in the kitchen. "Ole buzzard he fly away now—buzzard he fly away." I can't sing, but I can remember the way she sang it. It's funny how things stick in your head.

Eva had her head on my shoulder and my arms were around her. But we were as far away as Brooklyn and New York with the bridges down. Somebody was making love, but it wasn't us.

"When's he coming?" I said, finally.

"He's drivin' up in his car," she said. "He started yesterday."

"Young Lochinvar complete with windshield," I said. "He ought to be careful of those roads. Has he got a good car?"

"Yes," she said. "He's got a right pretty car."

"Oh, Eva, Eva," I said. "Doesn't it break your heart?"

"Why, honey," she said. "Come here to me."

We held each other a long time. She was very gentle. I'll remember that.

I stayed up most of that night, finishing revision on the novel. And, before I went to sleep, Furfew came to the house on the river plantation and walked in. I was standing in the hall and I couldn't lift a hand to him. So then I knew how it was going to be.

He came in the flesh, next afternoon. Yes, it was a good car. But he didn't look like Benedict Arnold. He was tall and black-haired and soft-voiced and he had on the sort of clothes they wear. He wasn't so old, either, not much older than I was. But the minute I saw him beside Eva, I knew it was all up. You only had to look at them. They were the same kind.

Oh, sure, he was a good business man. I got that in a minute. But, underneath all the externals, they were the same kind. It hadn't anything to do with the faithfulness or meanness. They were just the same breed of cats. If you're a dog and you fall in love with a cat, that's just your hard luck.

He'd brought up some corn with him and he and I sat up late, drinking it. We were awfully polite and noble in our conversation but we got things settled just the same. The funny thing is, I liked him. He was Young Lochinvar, he was little Mr. Fix-it, he was death and destruction to me, but I couldn't help liking him. He could have come to the island when Eva and I were married. He'd have been a great help. I'd have built him a house by the cove. And that's queer.

Next day, they all went out in the car for a picnic, and I stayed home, reading my novel. I read it all through—and there was nothing there. I'd tried to make the heroine like Eva, but even that hadn't worked. Sometimes you get a novelty like that—it looks like a world-beater till you get it into production. And then, you know you've just got to cut your losses. Well, this was the same proposition.

So I took it down to the furnace and watched it burn. It takes quite a while to burn four hundred sheets of paper in a cold furnace. You'd be surprised.

On my way back, I passed through the kitchen where Serena was. We looked at each other and she put her hand on the bread- knife.

"I'll like to see you burning in hell, Serena," I said. I'd always wanted to say that. Then I went upstairs, feeling her eyes on my back like the point of the bread-knife.

When I lay down on the bed, I knew that something was finished. It wasn't only Eva or the novel. I guess it was what you call youth. Well, we've all got to lose it, but generally it just fades out.

I lay there a long time, not sleeping, not thinking. And I heard them coming back and, after a while, the door opened gently and I knew it was Eva. But my eyes were shut and I didn't make a move. So, after another while, she went away.

There isn't much else to tell. Furfew settled everything up— don't tell me Southerners can't move fast when they want to— and the packers came and four days later they all started back for Chantry in the car. I guess he wasn't taking any chances, but he needn't have worried. I knew it was up. Even hearing Cousin Belle had "come around" didn't excite me. I was past that.

Eva kissed me good-by—they all did, for that matter—the mother and the three sisters. They were sort of gay and excited, thinking of the motor-trip and getting back. To look at them, you wouldn't have said they'd ever seen a bill-collector. Well, that was the way they were.

"Don't write," I said to Eva. "Don't write, Mrs. Lochinvar."

She puckered her brows as she did when she was really puzzled.

"Why, honey, of co'se I'll write," she said. "Why wouldn't I write you, honey?"

I am sure she did, too. I can see the shape of the letters. But I never got them because I never left an address.

The person who was utterly dumbfounded was Mr. Budd. We camped in the house for a week, getting our own meals and sleeping under overcoats—the lease wasn't up till the first and Furfew had made an arrangement with the owner. And Mr. Budd couldn't get over it.

"I always knew they were crazy," he said. "But I'll never get such cooking again." I could see him looking into a future of boarding-houses. "You're young," he said. "You can eat anything. But when a man gets my age—"

He was wrong, though. I wasn't young. If I had been, I wouldn't have spent that week figuring out three novelties. Two of them were duds, but the third was Jiggety Jane. You've seen her—the little dancing doll that went all over the country when people were doing the Charleston. I made the face like Serena's at first, but it looked too lifelike, so we changed the face. The other people made most of the money, but I didn't care. I never liked the darn thing anyway. And it gave me a chance to start on my own.

They couldn't stop me after that. You're harder to stop, once you get rid of your youth. No, I don't think it was ironic or any of those things. You don't, outside of a book. There wasn't any connection between the two matters.

That fall I met Marian and we got married a year later. She's got a lot of sense, that girl, and it's worked out fine. Maybe we did have the children a little quick, but she'd always wanted children. When you've got children and a home, you've got something to keep you steady. And, if she gets a kick out of reading love stories, let her. So I don't have to.

In a book, I'd have run across Eva, or seen Furfew's name in a paper. But that's never happened and I suppose it never will. I imagine they're all still in Chantry, and Chantry's one of those places that never gets in the news. The only thing I can't imagine is any of them being dead.

I wouldn't mind seeing Furfew again, for that matter. As I say, I liked the man. The only thing I hold against him is his moving them back, that way, before the lease was up. It was all right and he had his reasons. But they had two weeks left—two weeks till the first. And that would just have finished the year.

And when I get to sleep nowadays, Marian's there in the next bed, so that's all right, too. I've only tried to go back to the river plantation once, after a convention in Chicago when I was pretty well lit. And then, I couldn't do it. I was standing on the other side of the river and I could see the house across the water. Just the way it always was, but it didn't look lived in. At least nobody came to the window—nobody came out.

No Visitors

(1940)

WHEN THE MAN in the bed woke up, it was early in the afternoon. He had learned, some weeks before, that it was a good thing, when you woke up, to hold yourself perfectly still for a moment, until you were wide awake. In that way you wouldn't make an unexpected movement and the pain, if any, wouldn't jump at you. It was the jumping at you that mattered—if you merely lay still and let it seep into you, you could stand it quite nobly and heroically, even if no one else were around. But this afternoon there was nothing—just a 'little whisper, a little reminiscence—nothing real. Just enough to make you conscious that there had been a great deal of it, once. It was wonderful.

"Boy!" said John Blagden to himself. "You're going to get well. Do you know it? You're going to be O.K."

He sat up a little higher in bed and listened to the sounds of Floor 7. The radio was on as usual, next door, at "No Visitors," muted and throbbing—the old guy across the hall was getting a different program. "Now, Lucy Lee, don't you worry—we'll get them cows back for you." It was a little loud, but John Blagden didn't mind. The old guy was just a mild heart case—let him amuse himself. When you'd had a McWhirter, with adhesions, you could afford to be generous to people like that.

As he often did, when he waked up, he had a sense of the whole big mechanism of the hospital, cut off from the rest of the world, yet self-sufficient, like a boat or a train. That was a hang-over from the dreams after the operation. But it made an amount of sense. There was a routine, with fixed stops, and you saw a great deal of people you would probably never see again. Sometimes you didn't even see them—just knew them as you knew his neighbor, No Visitors, from a card stuck in a door and a radio heard through the wall. Nevertheless, he had been able to build up a pretty good picture of his neighbor. She was small and faded and whiny, and she put on a bright pink bed jacket before the doctor came. She didn't like Orson Welles, but she just loved Nelson Eddy and, though she complained about the food, she didn't want to die. He wondered if she had any children—there was probably a toothy, successful son somewhere. The grandchildren weren't brought to see her, because she'd cry at them. But the son sent flowers on Monday, and she talked to the nurses about him. Yes, that would be it. Afterwards, when it was over, the marcelled daughter-in-law would talk about mother's illness to her friends, with a proprietary pride. "Ed had everything possible done—you know how generous Ed is!" No, he couldn't really like No Visitors. But it must be tough, being No Visitors, day after day.

He could do with a cigarette. When he stretched his arm for it, the shadow of pain increased by a fraction, but that had no significance. He lit the cigarette cautiously and inhaled. For the first time, it tasted right, not like hay and ether. He drew the smoke all the way inside him—inside his body that had been sick and was getting well.

"Have a nice nap?" said the nurse, coming in. "That's a good boy."

She smiled, professionally, and put cold fingers on his wrist, glancing at her watch. Some of their hands were warm and some were cold, but they were all nice girls, except for the one night nurse who had said she had no orders to give him the hypo, that time. He didn't even know what she looked like, but he had hated her for a long while. Now, it seemed silly to have hated her—indeed, silly to have hated anybody. *I'm Tiny Tim, himself and in person,* he thought. *But I don't mind.*

"How is it outside?" he said.

"It's cold," said the nurse, "but I like it cold. I'm from Vermont. A lot of the girls don't like it, but I do. Don't you want the bed up—you'll want to read your book, I guess."

She went to work, smoothly and efficiently, fixing the pillows, cranking the bed with the little crank, while he thought about her being from Vermont. As she bent to lift him, her black hair was neat under her cap and her body touched him, impersonally. It was funny, being taken care of by somebody you knew as well and yet as little as you knew a nurse. Must be funny for them too.

"All righty?" she said, smiling.

"All righty," he said. "Oh, look, would you just get me that board? I might do a little work."

"Did doctor say——" said the nurse.

"Oh, it's O.K. with Doctor Dennis." said John Blagden. "I've talked to him. Anyhow, I've got to start making some money or you'll throw me out for nonpayment of dues."

"I guess we're not worrying," said the nurse. "A famous author and everything." She shook her head. "You men," she said. "Always wanting to get back to your business. There's a very nice gall bladder in 735 and he keeps in touch with his office three times a day. But it's not so good for him—he's the fussy kind. Always fussing. I'd pull out his phone if I were Doctor De Lacey. Lucky I'm not, I guess."

"Am I the fussy kind?" said John Blagden, unable to help himself.

"No, you're a model patient. Only I'm not saying what model," said the nurse. It was, obviously, a routine jest.

John Blagden laughed obediently.

"That's what I always tell them," said the nurse, with satisfaction. "They're all model patients—only I'm not saying what model. It makes them see the humorous side of it."

"I can see it would," said John Blagden. He drew a breath. "Doctor Dennis didn't come in, did he?" he said, in a slightly altered voice. "I mean, while I was taking my nap."

The nurse shook her head. "No, doctor hasn't been on the floor since I came on," she said. "But he'll be in."

"He was going to look at my pictures," said John Blagden. "He and Doctor Seaver. So I was just wondering."

"Now, don't you worry about your pictures," said the nurse. "Any time Doctor Seaver operates, things are going to be all right." She spoke almost reprovingly. "Of course, they have to take the pictures afterwards," she said. "Just to check."

"All the same, he must lose some patients," said John Blagden, drawing on his cigarette. "I mean anyone must."

"Well, there was that poor old man—such a sweet old man," said the nurse. "But that was before you came in. Gee, that was a shame, though—I felt awfully sorry for his family. Such nice people. They were so appreciative, too—they knew Doctor Seaver had done everything he could."

"What was the matter?" said John Blagden.

"Complications," said the nurse, with a veil on her face. "But you don't have to worry. It wasn't a bit like yours." She looked at her watch. "Gee, I've got to hurry," she said. "I'm late now with my pulses. But if you want anything you know what to do."

"You bet," said John Blagden. He stubbed out the cigarette and lay back. It was fine to lie back, to carry on a normal conversation. It was fine to be able to talk about a nice old man who'd had complications and not have it worry you. In fact, everything was fine. He'd better call Rosalie and tell her so.

He lifted the phone, gave the number.

"Is Mrs. Blagden there? ... Oh, hello, Edna. ... Yes, this is Mr. Blagdcn.... Yes, I'm much better, thanks. ... All right, I'll hold on."

He waited, tasting the moment, while little footsteps went away inside the phone and something crackled. Then there was the warm, known voice.

"Hello, honey.... Oh, perfectly fine. I had a nap. Pete's coming in later to tell me about the pictures. And look, honey, don't try to come up this evening. It looks darn cold.... No, honestly, don't. Charlie may come in, and if he doesn't I'll just lie around and work. I think I've got a new slant on the chapter. How are the kids?"

He listened, talked and laughed. The warm, known voice told him the small familiar things—about Susan's being in the play and Bill's arithmetic. They were good to hear. He could see them all, living in the apartment without him, as if he were looking into a doll's house. They looked pleasant, a pleasant family. They had a dog and goldfish, a servant and food' on plates and lamps that turned off and on. The doll called Father wasn't there, right now, but that would get fixed, in time.

He'd never much thought of their being a family before never stood off from them to look. It seemed, in a sense, ridiculous that he, John Blagden, should have a family. As if he were pretending. And yet, they were there. They'd made something, he and Rosalie, something that wasn't just getting married and renting an apartment. They had done so, almost without thinking, and yet it was going to go on.

"'By, honey," he said. "Take care of yourself." He heard the warm voice, "'By, darling." *Yes, we've done it pretty well,* he thought. *Poor kid—this has been tough on her. She was scared, that night. I could see her being scared and not showing it. Well, we'll make it up, somehow. You're a lucky stiff, Blagden. You don't know how lucky you are. You might have had a wife like Jo Pritchett and children with web feet.*

He put back the phone and stared at the sheets of yellow paper on the board. It seemed a geologic age since he had last written words on yellow paper, but that, too, was going to be all right. He could see, now, that the last two chapters of the novel were bad—he must have been sick when he wrote them. But he had a new slant now, and could push ahead. He drew a few squiggles, a house with smoke coming out of the chimney and a bird with spotted wings. That was necessary, for some reason. Then he crumpled that piece of paper, threw it on the floor and began to write.

An hour later he put the pencil down. About five hundred words, maybe. Not much, but a start. And it came all right— it had left him tired, but it came. It was going to be a good book—maybe better than that. At forty-three, you ought to be able to write a good book, if you were ever going to. The old boys had. He saw deliciously and for a large, childish instant the long reviews, all saying the same thing. It didn't matter, it meant nothing; you wrote for a different reason—but, when it came, it was like honey on the tongue. He had had it just once before, for *The Years Are Bold,* eight years ago, and he was still known as the author of *The Years Are Bold.* But the new one was going to change that. He had the stuff to change it, now.

There was nothing like a blank sheet of yellow paper and a pencil in the hand—neither love nor health nor youth. There was nothing comparable. He supposed Pete Dennis got an equal kick out of medicine, but he did not see how Pete could.

Now the shadow of pain had strengthened, but you could

expect that, still, in the afternoon. You didn't get over a serious operation in a day or a week. Only now the docs knew what to do. *I suppose, fifty years ago I'd be dead,* he thought solemnly. It was good to be able to think of that quickly and without fear. He took out the thing in the secret part of his mind and looked at it. Yes, he had been afraid to die. Even talking offhandedly with Pete and in spite of the pain, it had come for a moment like a wave, the blind primal terror. He'd held on to Rosalie's hand. And then they'd given him the shot and you had to be a gentleman. But the terror had been there.

There was a knock at the door. "Mr. Fentriss to see you, Mr. Blagden." Then Charlie, a trifle hushed, as all visitors were, and not knowing quite what to do with the flowers. He was glad to see old Charlie, with his crisp, waxed moustache and his good suit.

"Well," he said. "You horse thief. Thanks a lot. They look swell."

"You look swell yourself," said Charlie. "I think you're faking." He sat down on the edge of a chair, as visitors did.

"Oh, I'm fine," said John Blagden. "It was just a little Mc-Whirter."

"A little what?" said Charlie.

"It's what they call it," said John Blagden, "when they cut a lot of you out and sew it together again. They found some adhesions, too," he said, with pride.

"And you were three hours on the table and the doctors said it was a miracle," said Charlie. He grinned. "I know," he said. "What I do for ten per cent! I her I've had more long-distance operations than any man in New York. Well, I'm glad it's over. We were kind of worried." His eyes brightened. "Done any work?"

"No, Simon Legree. But I'm going to."

"That's good," said Charlie. His waxed moustache bristled like a friendly cat's. "A couple of things came up," he said. "I haven't bothered you about them, but I just thought we'd run through them. TDS wants to do a version of *The Flowers That Bloom* on their workshop hour. They'll only pay a hundred—it's sustaining—but the hour's been getting attention, so I said all right." He paused. "Hank Lieber wants another Ma Hudgins story."

"I won't," said John Blagden. "I'm sick of Ma. And I want to get ahead with the novel."

"All right," said Charlie. "But they'll go up two hundred and fifty, and I had to ask you." His voice was sad.

"Tell them I'll think about it," said John Blagden. "In other words, tell them to hell with it, in a nice way."

"All right," said Charlie. "But I just thought, coming up here—well, suppose Ma Hudgins had an operation. You ought to have the background cold by now."

"Body snatcher!" said John Blagden, with affection. "Tell them I'll think about it."

"All right," said Charlie, "but just remember, if you do, it establishes the new price. Now——"

He went on; John Blagden listened and answered. It was good to talk about work, to hear that this was a hit and that wasn't doing so well—to get back into the familiar, smoky world of shop-talk and publishers' gossip and contracts and prices. At the end, Charlie rapidly told three funny stories, picked up his neat hat and neat overcoat and left, with an unexpected "When you're over this, you'll feel a lot better, fella. I did, after my bust."

"I never knew you had a bust," said John Blagden.

"That was when you were in England," said Charlie. "They had to give me two transfusions. But I've taken a lot better care of myself ever since. Well, I'll call Rosalie and tell her you're just a big bluff."

He left, and John Blagden thought about Ma Hudgins. Charlie was right, as Charlie generally was. *Ma Hudgins Goes to the Hospital* was a definite story, worth a definite price. He was sick of writing Ma Hudgins stories, but he could begin to feel the plot form in his mind. Well, plenty of time.

The orderly came in.

"Afternoon, Mr. Blagden."

"Afternoon, Jim." He rolled over, gingerly. He didn't ask what his temperature was—only new patients did that and he was an old inhabitant. When the orderly had gone, however, he wondered. There might be a little temperature—just a little. The bed felt scratchier and less comfortable than it had an hour ago. But, even if there were a little temperature, it didn't matter. He closed his eyes.

When he opened them again, the room was dark and there was a presence at the door. "Hello," he said, with a thick tongue,

"Hello, Jack," said Pete Dennis. "Did I wake you up?"

"Nope," said John Blagden. "I wasn't really sleeping. Come in, Pete, and switch on the light."

Pete came in, as always, diffidently. He had dull red hair and a pleasant, ugly face. His white coat was a little rumpled, but it suited him. He sat down in a chair, looking big for it.

"Well," he said, "what kind of day has it been?"

"Oh, fine," said John Blagden. "I even did a little work."

"On the novel?"

"Yes."

"That's fine. Lord!" said Pete Dennis, "I don't see how you do it. When I even have to write a report, I sweat."

"It's a gift," said John Blagden, smiling. "Just naked genius." He leered at his friend. "I'm going to do a Ma Hudgins about a hospital. The hero will be a man in white."

"Oh, for God's sake!" said Pete Dennis, with patient despair.

"Charlie suggested it," said John Blagden. "It won't be very bad. You'll be a clean-eyed young idealist, but you won't have to discover the secret of cancer or anything."

"Thanks," said Pete Dennis. His voice sounded friendly but absent, and a small cold wave went over John Blagden's skin.

"Well," he said, very casually, "did you look at the pictures?"

"Yes," said Pete Dennis, "I went over them with Seaver." He paused. "We went over the last tests, too," he said. "It's nothing to worry about, Jack. But, talking it over, we decided we might have to go in again."

"You decided what?" said John Blagden, in a voice of complete incredulity. He could feel the pain jump at him now.

"I told you I was keeping my fingers crossed," said Pete Dennis. "Sure, I'd rather it had happened the other way. But, every now and then you get a different situation—well, I told you about that."

There was a small silence in the room.

"A doctor!" said John Blagden, breathing deeply. "A doctor! I wouldn't trust you to poison a dog!"

"Go ahead, if it helps," said Pete Dennis. His head was heavy and averted the dull red hair shone under the bright light. The big body looked tired and worn. *It's what he always does,* thought John Blagden—*my God, it's my having to cheer him up when he was an intern! It's what makes him a good doctor, I guess.*

"Sorry, Pete," he said. "I didn't mean that at all."

"That's all right," said Pete Dennis, hurting himself. "You've got every sort of right. And I told Seaver I'm not going into it bullheaded. I want to have Abbott take a look at you."

"I—don't—need—a—consultation," said John Blagden slowly. "If you and Seaver——"

"I want to have Abbott look at you," said Pete Dennis inexorably. "He's about the best man in the country. He'll be in tonight—it just happens he's down here for a meeting and I got him on the phone. You needn't worry about the bills," he said quickly. "Abbott's very decent. It's just that we'd feel a little surer."

"Oh, I won't worry," said John Blagden. "I won't worry at all." He laughed sharply.

"Listen, Jack!" said Pete Dennis firmly. "In the first place, if Abbott doesn't think so, we won't do it. In the second place, even if he does, we're not shooting in the dark. It's a perfectly well-known operation. If you want to know about it techni-cally—"

His slow, reassuring voice continued. John Blagden listened, not listening.

"All right," he said, at the end. "You're the doctor."

"You'll like Abbott," said Pete Dennis earnestly. "Don't get put off if he talks to you about eighteenth-century chamber mu-sic. He knows his stuff."

"Okay," said John Blagden. "And, by the way, when will you cut?"

"Depends on Abbott," said Pete Dennis, his face still heavy and averted. "But don't worry. We won't rush you."

"That's a good idea," said John Blagden. He began to talk quickly. "Look here, Pete," he said, "you know I believe every-thing you've said. But you've got to give me a little time, that's all. I mean, it's only sensible to take precautions. Well, for instance, I haven't made a will since Bill was born. And that throws things out in New York State. I can get Jimmy Williams up tomorrow and fix it."

"We-el," said Pete Dennis, "if it makes you feel any better—"

"Of course it does," said John Blagden. "I mean it's a sensible precaution. I'd do it if I were having my appendix out. I ought to have done it before." He breathed deeply. "How much chance is there, Pete?" he said. "I've known you long enough—you ought to be honest."

Pete Dennis made a sharp gesture. "Listen, Jack," he said, "there's a chance in every operation. There's a chance in having a tooth out. But—"

"Thanks," said John Blagden. "That's what I wanted to know."

"Don't be a fool," said Pete Dennis.

"I'm not," said John Blagden. "After all, I've been through it before. When's Abbott coming?"

"Oh, ten—ten-thirty—as soon as he's through with his meeting," said Pete Dennis in a relieved voice. He smiled his pleasant, ugly smile. "I'll be with him," he said. "He may show up in a tuck, but he'll know his business. And then, when he's through, we can really talk over the whole works." He rose. "Frances sent her best," he said. "She'd have been in to see you before, but she's had a cold. And, Jack, this is just a little setback. You've got to think of it that way. I won't have you thinking anything else."

"Check," said John Blagden. He watched the big shoulders swing out of the door. Old Pete. He'd first run into Pete twenty years ago. They'd drunk beer at Jerry's place, with a man who was dead and a man who had come to nothing and "Hooks" Wilson, the prof, who had had the scandal, later. And now Pete was a first-class doctor, and he was a well-known writer. But a doctor had it over a writer—he got nearer to the bone. If Pete said the operation was going to be all right, it was going to be all right.

His tray came in and he ate, keeping something at bay. When the tray was gone and he had joked with the nurse, it came back, not to be denied, the trained, automatic knowledge. A writers business was seeing and hearing—to note the tone and the inflection and mark them down on the wax record of the brain.

And, that being so, he had seen and he had heard. Pete was awfully good at his stuff, but he knew when Pete was worried about a case. He lay still, taking it, while two radios played.

It was not the fault of the doctors that the hospital had thin walls—they would have liked it otherwise, but an architect had designed the hospital. It was not the fault of the doctors that his body had to have another operation. It was nobody's fault. It just happened, and there it was, like a splinter of ice.

It had happened to Mr. Sherwood, down the line; it was happening, slowly, next door, at No Visitors. Mr. Sherwood had taken two days to die, quite noisily. There were times when everybody could hear him, even with the door shut. He had called for his mother, like somebody dying in a second-rate novel; he had carefully and loudly explained the interminable details of a business transaction in which he seemed to have been cheated by two brothers named Purvis. You could write a better death scene in your sleep—it was badly constructed and banal but, at the end, Mr. Sherwood had died; at the end, No Visitors would die. So that was that.

It would be a good idea to read, at this point, but he didn't feel like reading. If he hadn't been lazy this summer, he'd be two-thirds through his novel. If he hadn't had to do Ma Hudgins, it might be finished and in proof. Just as well. You couldn't die with a really good book unfinished, in spite of the people who had.

He switched on his radio—the station didn't matter. Out of humming and crackles, there came suddenly and authoritatively the bright, loving voice that was peace and solace to all mankind: "And next week, at the very same hour, we hope you all will be guests again at another of Aunt Mandy's Supper Parties, bringing you the glint and the glamour of old plantation days. Until then and with thanks to you, Kay Kibbey and your Jugtown Jugblowers and special thanks to you, Doris Delavan, for the haunting freshness you lend to the great songs of Stephen Foster—Aunt Mandy and Plantation Pork Products say to you-all, 'Good night! Keep a-smilin'!'"

The voice dwelt upon the last words, tenderly, richly, sorry to go. A gong struck. "It is now 8:30 P.M. by Hawkeye—H-A-W-K-E-Y-E—The timepiece of a nation," said another voice, with omen. John Blagden switched off the radio.

Yes, he thought. *It's eight-thirty p.m. The kids will be going to bed.* He discovered that his hands were damp. That had better stop. But it wouldn't help to turn on the radio again.

He saw, with the sharp eyes of fever, the bright, pleasant, lighted doll house—the life he and Rosalie had made. It wasn't so much to ask—just to keep that. But it wasn't a question of asking or denying.

He found himself thinking back, trying to find some logic in the pattern. There were all the priceless, worthless memories, from the look of the little silver cologne bottle on mother's bureau to kissing a yellow-haired girl named Rosalie Marsh in a taxi on 56th Street, without premeditation and for keeps. The memories included landscapes and furniture and people, they included poverty and Charlie Fentriss and the faces of two children and your name on the cover of a book. Together, they made up a life, and nobody else could ever know them all. There must be a logic and a pattern. But, instead, there were only gaps and flashes, like country seen at night from the window of a train.

A comfortable train enough, and you went along with it, with your pasteboard slip in your hatband. Until suddenly there was the destination—the stop called No Visitors. He could see it—a bare, wintry platform. Beyond it there was night and snow and the elemental cold. He could see a small John Blagden, getting down from the train to the platform and standing there, minute, lonely and afraid.

There was a knock at the door and John Blagden sweated. But it was only the black-haired intern who liked to be sociable. "Well, Mr. Blagden," he said, "getting along all right?" "Oh, fine," said John Blagden. He braced himself. "How did you like the show?" he said.

"I laughed my fool head off. He certainly knows his stuff, doesn't he?"

"George Crandall?" said John Blagden. "Yes, he's about as skillful as they conic. And, of course, Jimmy Trevor gives a beautiful performance."

"Do you know him?" said the intern, interestedly. "What's he like?"

"Oh, I've seen him around. Nice fellow very pleasant and modest. He married Betty Dunn—she's a peach. We've had them at the house."

It sounded gay and exciting, saying it. The intern looked impressed, which was as it should be. Go into your dance, John Blagden—tell some fascinating anecdotes about the world of letters. It's a nice youngster and it still thinks writers and artists are something special. If you asked it what dying was like, it would be very professional and no help at all.

"I remember when Betty was playing in 'Thar She Blows,'" said John Blagden. His hands were wet, under the bedclothes, but he told the anecdote with crispness and point. The intern laughed appreciatively. John Blagden wished that the intern would die or be called on the phone or anything that would get him out of the room, so a man could have peace. But none of these things ever happened and he knew they would not.

When the intern had left, John Blagden looked at his watch. About nine—almost nine. And Abbott might come at ten. Just about an hour. The train was going faster—he could feel it sway on the grades. Pretty soon, too soon, John Blagden would have to get down and stand on that bare, wintry platform. So what was there to do about it? ... Call Rosalie?... No.

A phrase, unbidden, flashed into his mind: "To prepare the soul for the great day." But if you didn't believe in things like that you didn't; no use faking. They didn't, most of the people he knew, though they went to church now and then, and were open-minded.

It's time for it, boy—for the consolations of philosophy, if any. You've been an artist and a modern and a free spirit. Well, you get what you pay for. Let's see what you've got. There's a novel and a half, five short stories, and a one-act play. "Among minor figures of the period"—yes. And I could have tried harder to get Tom Whitter into Chi Sigma, but I didn't. But that's washed up—I can't change it. I can't change being mean to Rosalie, that time. And a man should be judged by his work. We'll call it three short stories—we'll compromise for that. Dear God, if there is a God, save my soul, if I have a soul. Dear God, if there is a God, let somebody be reading my three short stories, sometime—somebody who isn't a Ph.D. with a thesis. And don't let poor Nelly starve. But that was Charles II and he didn't carry insurance. The insurance would take care of that end of it. At least, for a while, and better not think after that.

So it was all modern and scientific and well-arranged. You could die very nearly as privately in a modern hospital as you could in the Grand Central Station, and with much better care. And there would be the nice, kind drugs at the end—Pete Dennis would see to that. It all became part of a ceremony and, though you were the central figure, your lines didn't matter. No matter how badly you played the part, the notices would be favorable, on the whole.

His grandfather, the revivalist, had died shouting and praying in the black-walnut room at Englemere. He'd seen that and hated every minute of it, even as a child. It was phony, from first to last, with the family arranged in rows and Aunt Ellen leading the hymn. It was completely phony—it had had a fierce strength, which was gone. You could not summon back that strength, and yet there was nothing to replace it.

He was thinking very logically and clearly about the whole question. Yet, he must have dozed, for, suddenly, Pete Dennis was there in the room and there was a good deal more pain. The white-moustached, pink-faced little man with Pete Dennis had on a white coat as well, but you could see his stiff collar and black tie.

"Doctor Abbott?" said John Blagden. "It's awfully good of you to do this."

After the examination, John Blagden lay flat on his back. In the wall, the muted radio that belonged to No Visitors throbbed meaninglessly. He felt a sudden kinship with the sound. They'd be talking him over, outside, but he didn't much care what they said. You didn't, when it was decided. The porter was getting his bag now, and taking it to the end of the car.

"Save my soul, if I have a soul"—but it wasn't as simple as that. There remained the problem, and the question. For an instant, it seemed to him that he saw through the wall—saw into the next room, with its photographs on the dresser, and the small, faded woman in the bed jacket, playing her radio against the encompassing dark. It was a small soul, but so was his; so were all souls, raced with the fact. There was a community, somehow; it didn't really matter who you were.

Why, it's easy to do, thought John Blagden, with sudden surprise. *They make a great fuss about it, but its easy to do. It doesn't take a religion, or even a technique. All it takes is being mortal.*

He let go and had the pain come in. It was very considerable, but something remained untouched. That also would go, no doubt, with the drugs and the rest, but, while one had it, one had it. Having lived, it did not matter if you fumbled the last lines of the part.

"I am the resurrection and the life," said John Blagden, quoting. It did not matter now, if the words were true or not. They had been greatly said, though they were said for the living.

"Glad to meet you, No Visitors," said John Blagden. "Both members of the same club."

Then Pete came in, with his fine, poised smile, and the verdict written all over him.